I0664837

Readers love the Rose and Thorne series by JULIE LYNN HAYES

Bad Dogs and Drag Queens

"*Bad Dogs and Drag Queens* is a fun romp with two main characters that fit together like hand and glove."

—The Novel Approach

"This book is a fun read with lots of love…."

—Scattered Thoughts and Rogue Words

Civil War and Broken Hearts

"Vinnie and Ethan are adorably sweet together again."

—BFD Book Blog

Family Ties and Family Lies

"This really was an incredible read and I look forward to more in the future."

—Gay Book Reviews

By Julie Lynn Hayes

Love Wins
No Way Out
Yes, He's My Ex

ROSE AND THORNE
Bad Dogs and Drag Queens
Civil War and Broken Hearts
Family Ties and Family Lies

With M.A. Church
MOONLIT SKIES
Be My Alien
Be My Human

Published by Dreamspinner Press
www.dreamspinnerpress.com

No Way Out

Julie Lynn Hayes

DREAMSPINNER
PRESS

Published by

DREAMSPINNER PRESS

5032 Capital Circle SW, Suite 2, PMB# 279, Tallahassee, FL 32305-7886 USA
www.dreamspinnerpress.com

This is a work of fiction. Names, characters, places, and incidents either are the product of author imagination or are used fictitiously, and any resemblance to actual persons, living or dead, business establishments, events, or locales is entirely coincidental.

No Way Out
© 2018 Julie Lynn Hayes.

Cover Art
© 2018 Christine Coffee.
www.coffeecreatescovers.com
Cover content is for illustrative purposes only and any person depicted on the cover is a model.

All rights reserved. This book is licensed to the original purchaser only. Duplication or distribution via any means is illegal and a violation of international copyright law, subject to criminal prosecution and upon conviction, fines, and/or imprisonment. Any eBook format cannot be legally loaned or given to others. No part of this book may be reproduced or transmitted in any form or by any means, electronic or mechanical, including photocopying, recording, or by any information storage and retrieval system, without the written permission of the Publisher, except where permitted by law. To request permission and all other inquiries, contact Dreamspinner Press, 5032 Capital Circle SW, Suite 2, PMB# 279, Tallahassee, FL 32305-7886, USA, or www.dreamspinnerpress.com.

Trade Paperback ISBN: 978-1-64080-499-9
Digital ISBN: 978-1-64080-498-2
Library of Congress Control Number: 2018934256
Trade Paperback published August 2018
v. 1.0

Printed in the United States of America
∞
This paper meets the requirements of
ANSI/NISO Z39.48-1992 (Permanence of Paper).

To my good friend Nicole,
the true-life inspiration for my character of Nicole,
a true Marilyn Manson lover.

CHAPTER ONE

THE SILVER rims gleamed. The afternoon sun bounced off the highly polished surface, directly into Shylor's eyes. He never flinched, never showed his discomfort in any way. The muscles in his arms ached, and his shoulders threatened to spasm if they didn't receive a little relief from the relentless effort he'd been expending all morning.

But Shylor refused to give up. Failure was not an option with him. Failure came with its own consequences, and not of the pleasant variety. Was there a pleasant variety anymore? If so, that was so long ago he'd forgotten how good it might have felt. At the moment, all he could focus on was the potential for pain. The possibility of being reprimanded. And damned if he was going to let that happen. Especially over something as trivial as how he washed Randy's expensive set of wheels.

He wasn't aware he'd stopped moving until a cold voice from behind prompted him. "Don't stop until I tell you to." Icy fingers traveled down Shylor's spine—or what passed for one. He would have been hard put to find that anymore. Zoologically speaking, he could probably be classified as an invertebrate, something belonging to the order of cowards. Was there a special species known as weaklings? If so, he must rank somewhere pretty high among them, he figured.

He never turned, never acknowledged the rebuke. He knew it wasn't expected of him. He also knew what he would see, should he do so. Randy Grant. Six foot, silver hair that matched his expensive luxury sedan. Eyes of a changeable gray that reflected his mood and his pleasure. Sometimes they were tranquil seas that seemed almost an icy blue, and at those times Shylor could almost... but not quite... believe that Randy cared about him.

It was the other times, when the gray turned into dark and turbulent clouds, that Shylor knew he was in for a world of pain, and at those times there was nothing he could do to ameliorate the situation. All he could do was grit his teeth and bear it, wait for the storm to pass.

Randy Grant was forty years old, twice Shylor's age. To the business world, he presented the image of a successful entrepreneur as the founder and driving force behind one of the city's most creative marketing agencies: Granting Your Wishes. They called him the Silver Fox, because of his prematurely gray hair, but on Randy it looked good. He had a smile that charmed the pants off everyone he met—figuratively and literally. And he had a body to die for. Well, he should—he worked very hard at maintaining it. Having the money for an expensive personal gym couldn't hurt anyone, and neither did having a personal trainer who supervised his exercise regime and a dietician who made sure he ate very well and very healthy. Shylor wasn't fooled, though. Randy controlled every move. He knew exactly what he was doing every step of the way, and he reveled in his control.

Inside the bedroom and out.

Shylor's labors were exacerbated in no small way by the presence of a foreign object nestled inside of him. He felt it whenever he moved, pressed against his channel, a constant reminder of Randy's dominance. Purple and ridged, the butt plug was designed to remind Shylor just who he belonged to, and what purpose he served in the scheme of things, even as it prepared him to be plowed later, at Randy's whim.

He supposed it could have been worse. At least Randy hadn't demanded he wear the one with the wolf tail. That one was a specialty item, particularly popular with fetishists and furries. Randy was among the latter. He'd had costumes specially made for both of them, and had devised elaborate scenarios for their use. Cosplay at its kinkiest.

Shylor had never met anyone like Randy. He had mesmerized him from the beginning, drawn Shy into his world, and into his bed. And now he was locked there, for all eternity.

After the things he'd done, who else could possibly want Shylor? Randy had made him untouchable as far as other men were concerned.

Shy no longer had a choice in the matter. If he ever had. Randy had been the first, and if he had his way, he would be Shy's last.

If Randy was pleased with the way Shylor washed his car, then later he would reap a reward. Namely, by being fucked with some modicum of consideration for his own pleasure. But if not, then it would be the kowtow-to-Randy show all the way, with no regard to Shylor's well-being or safety.

Although Shylor had a safeword, there were times when it was simply disregarded. And sometimes he forgot to use it, thinking why bother? There was no safety—there was only Randy and what he wanted. Nothing else mattered.

The sound of an engine drew his faltering attention to the street. Without thinking, Shy turned his head. They lived on a high-end cul-de-sac, and passing traffic was rare. Was he dreaming, or was that really a police car? Shy's heart beat faster. For just a moment, he felt his liberation was at hand. Perhaps someone had noticed… someone had made a call… someone cared….

He searched for a sign that the officer behind the wheel was seeking him, Shylor. The policeman never turned his head. All he could see of him was his profile. How strong he looked… how protective. Was he going to stop, pull into the driveway?

But no, the car reached the end of the street and traversed the circular turnaround. Heading back in the other direction, it quickly disappeared from view.

Only then did Shy realize what he'd done. He stiffened, bracing himself for the inevitable. He didn't know what form his punishment would take—retribution came in many forms, and Shy was familiar with them all.

His heart pounded, his breath coming in short gasps in anticipation. *Just do it. Get it over with. Please….*

He felt Randy move closer, waited for the pain.

An unexpected shadow fell across the sedan, coming from the wrong direction. From the street, not behind him.

Shy looked up in confusion.

"Is something wrong?"

3

A GUY could sure get used to living in a place like this. These weren't just houses—they were more like mansions to Wyatt Findley. Raised in a cluster of tightly packed brick homes in south St. Louis, he'd had little exposure to the sort of life that people enjoyed in more well-to-do sections of the city. But all of that was changing, and Wyatt was meeting people now he'd only dreamed of getting to know before.

Still, he had a long way to go before he became one of them.

In the meantime, he'd jumped at the chance to house-sit long-term for a friend of his mentor, Lukas Callahan. He didn't even need Lukas's reminder that a patron of the arts was a grand thing to have. Wyatt knew that, and so did every other student at the art institute he attended. He would have leapt at the opportunity, anyway, just to have a place all to himself. One where he wasn't crowded in with a gaggle of other up-and-coming artists, all vying for space in which to paint. He would have done it for that alone, but the homeowner had thrown in food, the use of one of his cars, and a generous stipend to boot.

Heaven, Wyatt decided. This was heaven.

The houses on this private cul-de-sac were widely spaced and few. He was surprised the street wasn't gated, but then it didn't lead anywhere and he'd come to realize that traffic was generally limited to the inhabitants. There were only five houses, two on either side and one at the end. The one he lived in was the second house on the left as you came down the street from the main thoroughfare.

He'd caught glimpses of the couple next door. They were older, probably retired. She liked to garden and spent a lot of time tending to her flowers and shrubbery. Wyatt had no idea what he did. So far the only visitors he'd seen were of the delivery variety.

The house at the end of the street was for sale, a magnificent Tudor, with a magnificent price tag. He'd looked up the listing online, out of curiosity, and couldn't believe the numbers that he saw. In this economy, that might be a difficult sell unless they brought down the asking price. But then, this kind of home was way out of Wyatt's league for quite some time to come, assuming he could ever afford it.

The first house on the right was also empty, but not for sale. Wyatt suspected the homeowner was away, perhaps on business. A pricey landscape company arrived on a regular basis, and what appeared to be either a caretaker or housekeeper or something.

That left the house directly across the street, the one with the two men. Two very different men.

Granted, Wyatt had only been in the neighborhood for a couple of weeks, so he wasn't exactly what you'd call an expert on them or anything. But he was confused about their dynamics. At first he'd assumed they were employer and employee. The younger man did all the work while the older one supervised. And then he'd decided they were father and son, considering the apparent disparity in their ages. But that illusion had been dispelled when he caught sight of the kiss. Not a fatherly kiss, by any means. Although it didn't exactly look romantic either. Why he thought that, Wyatt couldn't say.

Perhaps it was a certain stiffness in the older one's demeanor. Something that even from a distance seemed cold and forbidding.

Wyatt thought the older man was handsome, in a slick sort of Cary Grant way, minus the warmth. But the younger one... he was very cute. He had long blond hair that he sometimes wore in a tail at the nape of his neck. Wyatt couldn't tell eye color from a distance, but in his imagination, they were blue as a summer sky in St. Louis, and very expressive. He longed to see him closer up, to affirm his first impression. Maybe get to know him better. It didn't seem like he went anywhere. At least Wyatt never saw him leave the house, except in the company of the older man, whom Wyatt dubbed the Keeper.

Even if he was taken romantically, who couldn't use a friend?

Wyatt peeked through the living room window. There he was now. Correction, there *they* were. The blond was on his knees, scrubbing at the expensive sedan the Keeper drove. Come to think of it, hadn't he been doing that same thing a few hours ago? How long did it take to wash a car? And come to think of it, couldn't Mr. Fancy Pants afford to take it to the sort of car wash where they not only cleaned it inside and out, they detailed it to smell brand-new? Hell, they'd probably pick it up and deliver it for him if he asked.

So why was he making this guy do it?

Something shifted in his mind's eye, and now Wyatt visualized the blond in a slightly different scenario—on his knees, hands bound behind his back, head bowed in silent submission. What had brought that on? Was it because he was getting the impression that this Keeper was treating the younger man like some kind of slave?

Suddenly Wyatt had the irrational desire to release the blond from his imaginary bonds, to set him free. It was time he discovered the true state of affairs between them, if for no other reason than for his own peace of mind. Afterward, he'd laugh about the situation, and tell himself how foolish he was. And maybe work the encounter into a sketch or painting.

He took a quick glance in the mirror. His brown curls were unruly—what else was new?—and perhaps he had a few smudges under his dark blue eyes. He had a bad habit of rubbing at them when he was drawing, and he wasn't very good at cleaning up after himself.

No matter.

He quickly crossed the street, approaching the pair, frozen in their curious tableau.

He meant to say hello and introduce himself. Explain that he was staying across the street. But something went haywire in his brain as he gazed in utter fascination at the handsome man.

"Is something wrong?" he blurted out instead.

SHYLOR FELT his heart stop at those magic words. It took a few moments for him to realize the question had actually been spoken aloud. It wasn't the product of his usually overactive imagination. And once realized, he found he could not respond. The words were locked in his throat, held by five years of obedience tempered with discipline. More than five years, if you counted the years of his childhood.

Is something wrong? Only everything. And nothing.

Shylor quickly withdrew into his shell. He looked down at the car, focused his attention on that. Randy would deal with the newcomer. Randy would do what needed to be done. Whoever this was, he was just a passerby, a momentary intrusion into their lives. He'd get the answer to his question and be gone and that would be that. Shy had himself to think of, first and foremost. He felt the false hope die in his chest, and he scrubbed at the silver rim with renewed vigor.

"I'm sorry, do we know you?" Randy's voice was smooth and fluid. When he'd originally opened his marketing business, he'd done voice-overs for many of his first customers, radio and TV both, but he'd stopped doing that, as if it was beneath him.

Randy often used the royal *we*, even if it might appear to an outsider that he referred to himself and Shylor. Shy knew better.

"Probably not." The voice was amiable enough, with a pleasant timbre. Shy caught himself glancing up, against his better judgment. But only for a second, as the stranger held out his hand to Randy. Just long enough to see the man wasn't hard on the eyes, either.

"I'm Wyatt Findley. I'm house-sitting right across the street. For Mr. Masterson."

Shy knew Randy wouldn't shake hands with the man. He held himself aloof from most human contact. Shy almost snickered as he imagined Randy using his prissy voice. *Don't you dare touch me with that.* How he managed at work, Shy couldn't even begin to imagine. One of the perks of being the head honcho, he guessed.

"I didn't realize he'd left for Europe already." Randy sounded miffed. He hated to be the last to learn things. "I've seen his car here, I just supposed—"

"I'm using it," Wyatt explained. "He left it with me."

And that was that.

A hand touched Shy's shoulder, and then that same hand appeared in front of his face, as if it was being offered to him, and he couldn't help but see it as a lifeline. He started to reach for it but thought better of his action at the last moment and knocked an imaginary bit of dirt from the car's pristine panel.

"And you are?" Wyatt prompted.

Shy felt his face being tilted upward, and his heart pounded madly in his chest. Oh there would be hell to pay for this, no question.

"Sh-Shylor," he managed to stammer out. He could feel Randy's annoyance behind him, but he couldn't make himself look away.

"Is there something we can help you with?" Randy broke into the moment, and Wyatt released Shy's chin. He was quivering, which made the butt plug quiver too, and fresh waves broke through him. He fought against them, stifling a moan. Not the time or place. And if he dared to come, without permission....

"I was going to ask you the same thing. I noticed Shylor's been working on the car for a long time, thought he might like a hand."

"Shylor has everything under control. He's simply very thorough, that's all. Mr.... Finley, did you say?"

"No, *Findley.* With a *d.* Shylor, what do you say? I don't mind using a little elbow grease. Between us, I'm sure we can knock this out in no time."

Shylor stopped in midswipe, stared up at the good-looking brunet. Would Randy punish him here, right in front of this man? Humiliate him in some way? Or would he wait until they were alone inside the house to carry out his retaliation? That there would be some form of punishment, Shylor had no doubt. Whatever it was, he'd live through it. He always did.

To think, this guy was just across the street. Maybe they'd have to be more careful....

"I think the car looks fine. Shylor, you can be done."

To an outsider, Randy's voice was cold and emotionless, but Shy knew better. There was a rage building inside of him. One that would need to be expended in some way. But Randy would never let that be seen by anyone else. He had better self-control. He wore his mask well.

"Wonderful! I have an idea. Why don't you come over and I'll make us some drinks and we can get acquainted?"

"I'm afraid that's not possible." As usual, Randy answered for him.

Shylor dropped his eyes, feeling hope spin away. He wouldn't mind getting away from the house. That happened all too seldom anymore. And generally the places where Randy took him, when he did deign to take him anywhere, were clubs for people who enjoyed the same sort of lifestyle Randy did. And when they went to those places, Randy insisted on being addressed as *Master* or *Sir*, although that rule was not enforced at home.

Rules. Always about the rules. Until Shy had come to live with Randy, he'd never really lived by any. Since that time, he'd done nothing but.

"I see. You'll come over, won't you, Shy?"

So casual. So inviting. Visiting one's neighbors. That's what normal people did, didn't they? They got on with the people who lived around them, were friendly and helpful. Had actual conversations.

But Shylor didn't consider himself to be normal. He didn't deserve to have real discussions with real people. He didn't deserve anyone's friendship. And he knew he would never have it.

Everything he was, he owed to Randy. His self-worth was tied up in Randy's ownership. He belonged to Randy, and had ever since his mother had sold him to the businessman.

"I can't." He forced the words out stiffly.

Maybe his punishment would be lessened now.

Shy fought to control the trembling that threatened to overtake his limbs and exacerbate his current situation. The moment of hope had passed. Wyatt would go, and that would be the end of that. Randy would never allow him near again, that much Shylor knew. But he had other things to think about.

Like enduring whatever punishment Randy chose to inflict.

So caught up was he in thoughts of Randy's retaliation that the sound of Wyatt's voice startled him, and he froze in place.

"Well, another time then, Shylor."

Didn't he understand no when he heard it?

"That is, if your dad doesn't mind."

Oh. My. God.

Shy was conflicted. Part of him wanted to giggle so badly he could taste it—what he wouldn't give to sneak a look at Randy's face, which was undoubtedly very flushed. The other part was appalled. A bad situation had just become worse.

Let Randy explain the truth. Shy wasn't about to touch the subject for love or money. If asked, the best answer he could offer was "it's complicated."

"I'm not his father."

Oh yeah, Randy was upset. His voice had just assumed glacial proportions of the Titanic variety.

"Oh, sorry. I just assumed."

That was bound to help. Not.

Shylor didn't think Wyatt seemed sorry at all. In fact, he sounded rather amused. Shy wanted to see for himself. He knew better than to look, knew it wasn't in his own best interest. But, at this point, he was pretty well fucked anyway, so why not? He cocked his head slightly and peeked. Sure enough, Wyatt was grinning at him. Shy dared not offer a smile in return.

A fist bump was certainly out of the question.

Get out of here now, while the getting's good. A feeling of panic welled in his breast. He wasn't sure what Randy might do to Wyatt, provoked in that way. He knew Wyatt had no idea what Randy was capable of or he wouldn't taunt him like that.

"We have to go. Thank you for stopping by, Mr. *Fin*ley. Now, if you'll excuse us...."

This time, no doubt, the mispronunciation was deliberate.

Shy didn't need to be told twice. He scrambled to his feet, ignoring the vibrations from the butt plug that raced along his nerve endings. At least he could excuse the wet state of his shorts on his occupation and none would be the wiser.

"Have a nice day." Wyatt's voice was so cheerful, so good-humored. But why shouldn't it be? He could come and go as he pleased, couldn't he? Make his own rules. "See you later, Shy."

Shy warmed inside, but he never looked, never responded. He kept his eyes cast down, knowing Randy watched. Even so, he felt Wyatt's withdrawal as his shadow ebbed from view.

"Inside! Now!"

"Sh-should I put everything up first?" Even Shy's voice trembled.

"Yes! And be damn quick about it!" Randy snapped. "I'll be timing you."

For just a moment, Shylor dared to hope that Randy would restrict himself to verbal recriminations. Being yelled at, he could deal with. But Randy's next words put an end to that idea.

"I'll be in the Blue Room."

That did not bode well.

But there was nothing to be done for it. Before Randy had time to stalk to the front door, Shy was in motion, emptying the bucket he'd been using, rinsing out the rags and laying them out to dry. Rolling up the hose. He knew the drill, and he didn't dare deviate from it.

Shy wasn't sure what to expect when he opened the door to the Blue Room. Anything was possible. Taking a deep breath, he walked into the barren room, empty at the moment but for a single chair.

Randy was pacing back and forth, a sure sign of his agitation. "Father? Ha! If he only knew… if he could only see." He stopped and pointed one well-manicured finger toward Shy. "You know the rules. You do *not* talk without permission."

Shylor nodded. He'd discovered years ago that debating any point only produced more pain.

"How dare he? How dare *you*? Ungrateful little bastard." Randy darted toward him, his slap landing full across Shy's cheek. Unprepared, Shy's head bounced back. His long blond hair flew into his face, but he made no move to brush it aside.

"Strip," Randy commanded in a heated voice, and Shylor hastened to obey, carefully setting every piece of clothing aside. He didn't want to give Randy any more of an excuse for violence than he already had. While he got undressed, Randy left the room, returning quickly, and not empty-handed.

When he spotted the rope, Shy knew it was going to be one of those nights. The only question was what position would he be tied in, and what would Randy choose to do to him then?

Randy wound the rope around Shy's wrists, then dragged him to the chair, yanked on the rope, and forced him to sit. He suspended Shy's hands behind the chair until they just touched the edge of the seat. Shy's back strained unnaturally across the top of the chair, taut as a bowstring as Randy trussed him, running the rope in a loop about his neck, and then down the front of his body.

Shy wondered what Randy had in mind. Usually he tied him the other way, to allow himself access to Shylor's hole. This way, even with his ass suspended over the seat, Shy didn't see that working out. So what then?

Randy reached beneath Shy and pushed against the plug. Shy shivered. So he was leaving that? Randy slid a cock ring over Shy's hardness and stroked it roughly. Then he slid the blindfold into place, and Shy's world went dark.

Now it would come. The beating… the whipping… the fucking… whatever Randy decided to mete out, even if Shy couldn't see it coming. He held his breath and counted….

"Think about your transgressions. I'm going out."

The door slammed, and silence fell.

CHAPTER TWO

MORE THAN a week went by before Wyatt was able to turn his attention to the strange case of Shylor and Randy across the street. Not that he'd forgotten about Shylor. Far from it—the blond occupied a large percentage of his waking thoughts. But real life had a cruel way of intruding itself. Wyatt was kept fully occupied, what with final exams, preparing his portfolio in hopes of receiving a showing, and dealing with a broken pipe in the kitchen, which had burst in the middle of the night and made quite the mess. Tests and painting and plumbers, oh my!

The same night he'd met the strange couple, Wyatt had noticed the car that Shylor had labored over for so long was missing from the driveway. Randy must have taken Shy out. That was something, he supposed. A reward for all his hard work. Even if the poor guy had to spend it in the company of the unpleasant older man. Randy had certainly not made a favorable impression on Wyatt... but Shy had.

He'd noticed, when they first met, that Shy's eyes were just as blue as he'd imagined they were. He'd held the color in his mind's eye, painstakingly mixing the paints on his palette until he recreated the exact shade.

Wyatt wanted to know more about Shy, learn what made him tick. He needed to know what the relationship was between those two. They had to be lovers, sure, that was more than obvious, but still.... Why were they even together? There must be a story there. Wyatt didn't feel any love vibrations between them, and that concerned him. Granted, he'd not spent all that much time as an observer of their situation. Perhaps he was jumping to conclusions.

Gut instinct told him he wasn't.

He wanted to bring a smile to Shy's face, ease the strain he saw there, bring him a bit of genuine joy. Or even a whole lot. But how could he with the Keeper maintaining such a tight rein on him? Was that a public face he wore, and perhaps in private he relaxed, and things were more agreeable, less tense?

Wyatt wanted to believe that was true, but his head screamed at him that something just wasn't right there. Call it his artist's instinct. That thing that helped him see what others didn't. He'd been a student of human nature too long, attempting to bring it to life on his canvas, not to have gained some insight. And all his senses told him Randy wasn't what he seemed to be, and that life in the house across the street was skewed in some way.

Well, common sense told him the man had to work sometime, didn't he? Of course he did. Wyatt would bide his time and strike when the moment was right.

The following Wednesday, Wyatt rose and made himself a pot of coffee. Not having any more classes until the summer session was a welcome break. He sat in the kitchen, sipping at the liquid heat, listening to an early-morning talk show on the radio. Normally he enjoyed the scathing humor of the two hosts, who often played against one another and spun tunes between witty repartee. But when one of them joked about there being rain in the forecast, Wyatt decided maybe he'd cut the grass before he couldn't. Good old St. Louis weather. Turn your back on it and it changed. Not always for the better.

The homeowner, Mr. Masterson, had a zero-turn lawn mower in the detached garage at the back of the house that was almost brand-new. It was a sweet ride. Wyatt enjoyed the orderly progression of its finely honed blades as he cut the lush zoysia into aesthetically pleasing rows, following the contour of the yard. It gave Wyatt a chance to get some fresh air, as well as the illusion he was exerting himself physically, while a myriad of pictures turned over in his mind.

Every single one of the images had bright blue eyes and a heart-stopping smile. He just knew if he could coax Shy into smiling for him, the result would be spectacular. Worthy of a painting.

What he wouldn't give to be able to put such a vision on canvas.

He finished cutting the grass before any sign of precipitation raised its ugly head. Wyatt brushed his arm across his forehead, wiping at the sweat he'd worked up. Glancing across the street, he realized the sedan was missing.

His chance was now. Should he take it?

Hell yeah. But first, he needed to rid himself of the stank of perspiration. He jumped into the shower and quickly scrubbed away the offending grime, then toweled off. Trying not to overthink things, he settled for a pair of camel shorts that he knew were flattering to him and showed off his slender legs, and a favorite T-shirt emblazoned with the image of Leonardo da Vinci.

He ran a quick brush through his curly mop, figuring it would dry well enough on its own, shoved the house key into one pocket, his wallet in the other, and locked the door behind him. Just as he started down the front walk, a familiar melody wafted toward him. Wyatt had to smile. He'd know that music anywhere. The ice cream man was coming.

That was it! He snapped his fingers at the scathingly brilliant idea he'd just had. It seemed forever until the large colorful truck turned down his street. Probably got held up by the children on the next block, wanting their own creamy treats. But it approached at last. Wyatt was the only person waiting for it. No surprise there.

"What'll you have?" the driver asked.

Not knowing Shy's preference, Wyatt bought two cones—one chocolate, one vanilla, to be safe. He had just enough change to cover his purchase. He thanked the vendor and crossed the street with confidence.

An artist bearing gifts.

He approached the door, juggled the cones and rang the bell, then waited.

SHYLOR WAS responsible for keeping the house spotless, despite the fact that Randy could well afford to have a housekeeper. But he pushed the duties off onto Shy, who reasoned that it was a privacy issue. Randy didn't want anyone to see the Blue Room or any of his assorted toys.

The trainer's name was Tony, and he came twice a week, on Randy's schedule, and never went beyond the decked-out gym in the lower level, which had its own entrance at the rear of the house.

The dietician, Joanna, was a tight-lipped young woman who seldom showed up in person, sending her menus to Randy by email. Her meals were strictly portioned, every calorie accounted for. It was up to Shy to see they were cooked to Randy's satisfaction. Shy didn't care for the regimen, didn't see any reason he should follow such a diet, but he didn't question Randy's orders. Those were the rules, and he obeyed them.

Despite his best efforts to put him out of his mind, Shy's thoughts often returned of their own volition to the handsome man who lived just across the street. Wyatt Findley. The name rolled off Shy's tongue when he daringly whispered it to himself. In Randy's absence, of course. Although he was sure they'd never be allowed to see one another again, he couldn't stop thinking about him. In his mind's eye, Shy dressed him in white armor, seated him upon a prancing black steed with blazing eyes. Made him into someone who'd carry Shy away, release him from his prison of shame. A prison of his mother's making.

But such daydreams were futile and only led to an ache in his heart that nothing could assuage, not even the furtive touches of his own hand, secretly masturbating in the bathroom to the image of Wyatt. Scouring any trace of his actions afterward, carefully masking the telltale scent with the bleach Randy insisted he use. Putting Randy's rules to good purpose.

The night they met was still fresh in Shy's mind. Time had crawled with infinite slowness as he'd been tied to the chair, unable to move, the butt plug in place as a reminder of what his purpose in life was. To pleasure Randy. To be ready for him whenever Randy wanted him. To wait through the times when he did not. Such as tonight.

At first he figured Randy would leave him tied up for a short while to drive home the lesson, then come back and fuck him hard. Any moment he expected to hear the key in the lock of the Blue Room, feel Randy's presence, even if he couldn't see him, thanks to the blindfold.

But he didn't return. After a while, Shy realized he wasn't going to. At least not for a good long time. This was his punishment. If he was lucky, it wouldn't get any worse. There were far more awful things than being tied up.

Shy dozed off and on during the night, but never for long, invariably startling himself awake. His muscles ached, and he longed to stretch them, to find another position, but that was impossible. He was helpless until Randy chose to return. And even then....

What if he didn't return? Shy pushed the thought aside as ridiculous. No way would Randy abandon his house and his possessions. They meant too much to the older man. And Shy was one of those possessions. Randy would not allow him to come to harm—he had too much time and energy invested in his training.

Had Randy ever loved Shy? At first, Shy had deluded himself that was the case. But now? Not so much.

But what if something happened while Randy was out? What if someone broke into the house? Would the intruder free Shylor or take advantage of his helplessness to loot the house? Or, worse still, what if the house caught fire? Shy would be unable to do anything other than go up in flames.

Would that be his chance for freedom?

Reality hit home when Shy was awakened from a fitful sleep by the sound he'd been anticipating, and a drunken Randy had stumbled into the room, demanding Shy service him. He'd fumbled with the knots, releasing him. Shy fell from the chair, his limbs unable to respond, despite Randy's belligerent orders. Randy had kicked him when he didn't immediately leap to attention, and Shy bore the blows without complaint. Once the blood returned to his extremities, they'd gone to the bedroom. He went down on Randy, and pretended that it was Wyatt he held in his mouth, Wyatt whose cock he gave pleasure to.

Without thinking, he whispered Wyatt's name into Randy's flesh as he felt him come. "What did you just call me?" Randy asked, and Shy held his breath in horror, but Randy rolled over and fell asleep without another word. The next morning, it was obvious he had no memory of the incident, and Wyatt's name never passed Shy's lips again. At least, not in Randy's presence.

He had just started the dishwasher when the doorbell sounded. Probably a delivery for Randy. Those weren't uncommon. Clients often sent gifts to the house. Randy welcomed them, although he was adamant about not allowing those same clients onto the premises. He wined and dined them elsewhere. A favored few even received invitations to Randy's favorite clubs. At those times, he frequently commanded Shy's presence, and he would accompany Randy and do whatever he told him to do.

He opened the door, expecting to see the retreating back of a delivery driver in brown uniform—they didn't require signatures and seldom waited to acknowledge receipt—but was startled to find the object of his wet dreams standing on his doorstep, bearing two ice-cream cones, wearing a sunny smile.

Shy's heart stopped, his eyes widened in panic. Oh God, what if Randy came home....

"Get out of here," he whispered in desperation.

OF ALL the reactions Wyatt had anticipated on his short trek across the street, hearing Shy tell him to go away wasn't one of them. Shy looked so... afraid... but why? Was Randy's hold on him so tight he feared Shy even talking to another person? Or was it Wyatt in particular?

Wyatt was confused. Especially when he saw the furtive look Shy gave to the ice creams in his hands, which, almost forgotten, were dripping onto the front stoop.

He was reminded of a game he'd played as a kid, with some of his friends, the object of which was to figure out what someone was looking at. "I spy with my little eye," the familiar chant went, followed by a guess of some sort. Wyatt thought he spied naked fear in Shylor's eyes. And he didn't like it. Not one little bit.

Wyatt was too startled to make an immediate reply, and Shy made no move to leave, so they remained frozen in an odd tableau, their gazes locked upon one another, as if each was mesmerized by the other. Wyatt could almost feel the indecision that pulsed between them. Surely he wasn't mistaken in thinking Shy wanted to talk to him as badly as he wanted to talk to Shy. If he didn't, wouldn't he have closed the door by now?

At least, that's what his intuition told him, although he was woefully ignorant of how to handle a situation like this, having never found himself in one before. What in the world could make someone look so scared? Wyatt wasn't sure he wanted to know. And yet he wanted to help Shy in any way he could. Clear his beautiful blue eyes, make him smile... free him from whatever held him in such a tight grip of panic.

"It's just ice cream. I thought you might like to share some with me. You like ice cream, don't you?" Wyatt was babbling. He wanted to get Shy to relax, but it didn't look like that was happening any time soon.

Um, think, think... do something.

He blindly thrust one of the cones forward. Did Shy's hand twitch, just for a moment? Did he start to reach for it and then hold himself back?

But why? Why in the name of all that was holy was he so damn afraid? And of what?

At the sound of an engine, Wyatt thought Shy was going to faint. His eyes grew bigger, and he looked about as bloodless as a vampire on a day pass. Wyatt turned toward the street. It was just the backfire of the mail truck, making its appointed rounds. Nothing there to be alarmed about. But as he pivoted back to tell Shylor so, the door slammed shut, leaving a stunned Wyatt gaping at it.

SHY LEANED against the door, his heart beating erratically, his hands clenched into fists. Despite his best efforts, he felt warm tears prickle in his eyes. No, dammit, no. It was better this way. What if... what if that had been Randy? The thought didn't bear contemplation. Shy had gotten lucky, no sense in tempting fate. No matter what his traitorous body was telling him to do. Open the door. Invite Wyatt in. Take the ice cream and feast on it. Oh damn, when was the last time he'd eaten ice cream? He no longer remembered. Months, at least. A punishment so longstanding he no longer recalled the crime he'd committed. And it didn't matter anyway.

It wasn't just the ice cream that was so dangerous, it was the way Shy found himself reacting to Wyatt. He'd never had this happen before, and he found himself shaken to the core with the strong desire threatening to topple his very existence. He didn't even understand why he wanted Wyatt so badly, he just did. Maybe because he seemed kind. And kindness was definitely lacking in Shy's diet.

Wyatt seemed sweet, and thoughtful, and he was good-looking.

The tears were closer to spilling now. Shy began to panic. If he gave in to this stupid emotional shit, his eyes would show it, and Randy would want to know why. And Shy wasn't a good enough liar to pull that off.

He was startled from his reverie, effectively halting his tears, by the reverberation of the door through his body. It took Shy a few seconds to realize Wyatt was knocking, followed by the sound of the doorbell as it echoed throughout the house.

Shy was torn. He could stand there and do nothing, wait for Wyatt to get the message and leave. He could run to his room, hide his head beneath the pillows and pretend he didn't hear. But what if Wyatt didn't leave? What if he stood there until Randy came home? Shy's stomach knotted at the very thought.

He forced himself to calm down, digging his nails into his palms to distract himself, so hard that small red crescents formed. He had to do this. He had to discourage Wyatt from ever coming over here, even if it turned out to be the hardest thing he'd ever done. And he'd done a lot of hard things in his short life.

But it was a matter of self-preservation. Even more, he didn't want Wyatt to be hurt, and there was no doubt in Shy's mind that Randy would hurt him.

He slowly opened the door, catching Wyatt in midknock, startling the other man.

"You can't be here," he whispered in as fierce a voice as he could muster. "He can't see you."

Wyatt processed the words.

Why didn't the fool leave, while he still could? He seemed ready to go, so go....

"Meet me somewhere" came Wyatt's unbelievable reply. "Tomorrow morning. Meet me somewhere else. Anywhere."

Shy felt bile rise in his throat. He swallowed quickly.

I can't... I can't... I....

"Where?" he almost sighed.

WHY DID Wyatt feel as if he'd just gained a major concession of some sort? As though the words came with a price? But that was silly, wasn't it? He pushed the thought aside, focused on Shy's question instead.

Where to meet? He hadn't honestly thought that far ahead. He'd blurted out the words as a reaction to Shy's attempt to push him away, which he didn't understand. But he wanted to understand. Very badly. There was a story there, one he wished to learn. He already suspected the answer involved Randy. His dislike for the pompous older man was only growing stronger.

"Where's good for you?" Maybe if he let Shy choose the venue, he'd feel more comfortable about meeting him.

Shy considered his answer. He seemed calm, but the rapid rise and fall of his chest belied his outward demeanor, as if he kept a tight rein on himself.

What in God's name was he so afraid of? And why did he keep peering behind Wyatt, as if he expected the devil himself to appear at any moment?

Maybe because he was afraid he might.

Just as Wyatt was beginning to think Shy had no intention of making a reply, he ran his tongue over his lips, took a deep breath, and murmured, "Shop for Less. Ten o'clock."

A grocery store? Confusion, tempered by disappointment, cascaded through Wyatt. Not exactly what he'd had in mind. Certainly not the place for intimate conversation of the getting-to-know-you variety. He looked into Shy's eyes, opening his mouth to protest, but something in those big blue eyes stopped him cold. "Shop for Less. Ten o'clock. I'll be there."

The next moment he was staring at the closed door once more. He could take a hint.

Well, now that he'd gotten his way he could.

No sense in pushing his luck. As spooked as Shy seemed, Wyatt didn't think it would take much to push him over the edge. As he turned away from the house, a small smile of satisfaction crept over his lips. He would have fist pumped in triumph but both of his hands were full. So much for his offer of ice cream. He could see Shy wanted it. So why didn't he take one?

"The game is afoot!" he announced in his best imitation of the inestimable Sherlock Holmes. Tomorrow couldn't come fast enough to suit Wyatt.

SHY PEEKED through the front curtains until Wyatt's retreating figure disappeared into the house across the street. Then he counted to ten quickly and rushed to remove any trace of the ice cream from the front step. Once he'd scrubbed it to his satisfaction, he hurried back inside and released a long breath of relief.

Okay, back to reality. What had he just agreed to, and why? Did he really say he'd meet Wyatt tomorrow morning at the grocery store? What had he been thinking?

He hadn't, that was the problem. At least not with his mind. He hadn't thought with his dick in so long, it had taken him by surprise. Not since those long-ago days when he'd been young and innocent, and thought Randy Grant was the answer to everything.

A violent tremor crashed through his body. He reached out, clutching the arm of a wingback chair for support. He forced himself to breathe through the panic until he felt secure enough to stand on his own.

What was done was done. He could hardly undo it—and he wasn't sure he really wanted to. The most important thing was to make sure Randy never found out. He had to put on the most convincing act ever. The best way to do that would be to remove thoughts of Wyatt from his mind, focus on the house and his chores.

Tomorrow had to remain his dirty little secret.

CHAPTER THREE

SHY'S LIFE was a regulated one. Randy had written a schedule for him that Shy copied onto the dry-erase board that hung in the kitchen. Every day had been assigned both general chores and specific ones. On Thursdays, Shy did the shopping. The dietician emailed Randy the menus for the following week the night before. Then Randy made up the actual list and printed it out. Shy was forbidden to deviate from it even one iota. No spontaneous purchases, nothing special for himself. He had to account for every penny spent. Randy scrutinized each receipt with an eagle eye. Even though he made good money, he was as tightfisted as they came, especially when it came to Shy.

The car that he allowed Shylor to drive was secondhand, an old Chevy compact, over fifteen years old. Nothing much to look at, but it was dependable, and it allowed Shy the freedom to run his errands. God forbid Randy allow him to use his car—that would never happen.

Shy could never park in the driveway, but was relegated to the back of the house, where the car couldn't be seen from the street. Shy didn't care. It was a mode of transportation, nothing more.

But today it was his ticket to paradise.

As he served breakfast, Shy was careful to maintain his carefully cultivated mask. He paid close attention to Randy's instructions, along with the list. Nothing he'd not heard before. After five years, it was the same old litany. But he pretended to hang on his every word.

Randy took another sip of coffee and grunted his satisfaction. Not that he'd think to praise Shy for it, or anything else. To Shy's dismay, he seemed to be in no hurry. Why today of all days?

Shy thought Randy would never leave. Usually quick out the door, today he lingered over his coffee, giving detailed instructions on his dry cleaning. Told a rambling story about his high school days that bore no relevance to anything. Finally he rose from the table with one last instruction—"Dinner at eight sharp"—and exited.

Once he'd gone, Shy checked his reflection in the mirror, retied his hair with a slender red ribbon, and stared into his own eyes.

Was he really going to do this?

If so, it was time to get dressed and go. Shy wasn't sure what to wear on a first date. He'd never been on one. Why was he even thinking of their rendezvous in this way? This was no date. It was a first and last meeting, nothing more. He hoped at least he'd come away from it with some memories to hold on to. He deserved nothing more. Other guys had first dates and first kisses, hopes and dreams and a future to look forward to.

Shy wasn't one of those.

He hadn't intended to dress any differently, until he stared at himself in the mirror and noticed with some surprise that he had. Dark gray slacks, and a lightweight polo shirt in a blue that Randy uncharacteristically had said matched his eyes. One thing he could say for Randy, he dressed Shy up pretty on the rare occasions when he took him out.

Shy grabbed the list and the car keys, muttered, "Ready or not, here I come," and locked the house behind him.

WYATT HAD been sorely tempted to suggest they ride together. Hell, they lived right across the street from one another. But common sense dictated if it was that easy, they wouldn't be meeting in a grocery store, would they?

He rejected most of his wardrobe as too casual. He had to make a good impression the first time—he suspected he might not get a second chance. So he donned his best gallery outfit, the one he used to wow the patrons who showed up to view his art up close and personal, hopefully to purchase it. Tan slacks and a long-sleeved light blue button-down shirt. He knew he'd pay the price for wearing sleeves in this weather, but it looked good on him and darkened his blue eyes. If that meant suffering a little in the humid St. Louis heat, then so be it.

Shop for Less was a discount supermarket chain, with locations that dotted the Midwest and Northeast. In this economy, people needed to cut corners where they could. When Wyatt shopped for himself, he availed himself of their low prices, so he was very familiar with the nearest store.

As he pulled into the half-empty lot, Wyatt's heart rose into his throat. There was no sign of the silver luxury sedan. Had Shy backed out on him? He checked his watch. Ten o'clock precisely. He parked Mr. Masterson's car away from most of the others, near an older car, but not too close. Didn't want to take a chance on being hit with the door. Then he gathered himself together, grabbed a cart from the corral, and ventured inside.

The secret of the store's success was a limited selection of items at good prices. Wyatt also appreciated the small snack area where you could sit and enjoy a fountain soda and a sweet or salty snack. That would be a better place to talk than pushing carts about the store, chatting between pulling down cans of food.

Assuming Shy even showed up. Which at this point looked doubtful. Well, then, he'd just have to march across the street again and do something more drastic to gain Shy's attention, although he wasn't sure what. He didn't even know why he wanted to get to know the blond so badly. Something in his eyes drew Wyatt, though. There was something there Wyatt could not forget. He sensed a soul in distress, and he ached to relieve Shy's pain.

He had to find out what it was, first.

He carelessly threw more items in his cart. He'd figure out something to do with them later, assuming he actually checked out. Rounding the corner from one aisle to the next, he collided with another cart moving in the opposite direction. As metal hit metal, the jolt sent shock waves running along his arms. Glancing at the other driver, Wyatt bit back his sharp retort, replacing his frown with a smile. *He came!*

Damn, but he looked good. Looked even better without that silver-haired Simon Legree–type creep standing behind him.

Wyatt's smile blossomed across his face, growing broader by the second. To his gratification, he got a small smile in return.

That's a good sign.

Shy peered curiously into Wyatt's cart, perplexity creasing his blond brow. Then he began to chuckle. Wyatt followed his glance at the objects he'd tossed so mindlessly inside and had to smile himself. Black olives, anchovies, Italian dressing, canned frosting, and chickpeas sat side by side in discordant splendor.

"That'll make an interesting dish," Shy commented in bemusement.

"No doubt," Wyatt muttered. "Here, let me put this stuff up and I'll just walk with you. We can get a drink and something to eat. Maybe they have ice cream?"

Various expressions played across Shy's face, and Wyatt held his breath, wondering which would win out. There was something so very uncertain about Shy, as if he were teetering on the brink between one state and another. As if his very soul was in imbalance.

Finally Shy nodded and Wyatt hastened to replace everything as quickly as he could, before the blond changed his mind. He couldn't help feeling there was a victory in there somewhere, one he planned to hold on to for as long as he could. Once the errant items had been taken back to where they belonged, Wyatt returned to Shy.

"Here, let me push that," he offered. "That way you can get what you need easier." Since Shy didn't object, they switched places and continued down the aisle. Wyatt wasn't surprised that Shy had a list, one he kept checking.

A lot of low-fat items, he noticed. Maybe Randy was on a diet.

They didn't speak. Wyatt pushed the cart while Shy located the items on his list, carefully marking off each one once he placed it with the others.

"Checking it twice?" Wyatt quipped.

Shy gave him a quizzical look.

"You know. Like Santa Claus?" Wyatt felt his joke fall flat, but forged ahead anyway. "He's making a list, checking it twice." That produced a small smile and Wyatt felt emboldened. "Gonna find out who's naughty and nice."

The smile faded.

Damn, he felt stupid. Had he struck a nerve?

The next moment the mask was back in place, and Wyatt felt like the scum of the earth. *Be more careful*, he cautioned himself. *You're treading a fine line here....*

"Um, do you cook?" He quickly changed the subject. They stood in the meat department. Shy critically examined two packages of beef, comparing them. He selected one, set the other back. "Yes, I do all the cooking." He riffled through the chicken parts, eyeing the thighs and the drumsticks in particular.

"I love to eat, but I'm not much of a cook," Wyatt confessed. "I practically live on ramen most of the time."

"That's not good for you. Too much sodium."

"Yeah, well, it's cheap." Wyatt laughed. "Since I've been house-sitting, I'm eating better, I have to admit. Mr. Masterson isn't stingy at all with the food budget."

Did Shy wince, or did Wyatt imagine that? Damn, he seemed to be hitting every one of Shy's nerves today, clumsy oaf that he was. But it was difficult to know what might or might not set him off. And Shy wasn't exactly being forthcoming either.

Wyatt was determined to get through to him, no matter how long it took. He was a patient man. He had to be—art wasn't created in a day.

He held his tongue until he noticed that every item on the list had been marked off, then turned the cart in the direction of the snack area, which was empty at the moment. "What kind of soda do you drink?"

"I can't drink soda. Just water."

Wyatt tamped down on the desire to raise an eyebrow. "Oh, okay. Water it is. Want some chips with that? Popcorn?" he hastily amended. He was finally catching on. Healthy only. For whatever reason. "No butter, no salt."

Wyatt breathed a sigh of relief when Shy nodded. That was a start. They took the farthest table in the back and set the cart out of the way. Shy slid into the bench seat. Once he was fairly sure the blond wasn't about to bolt, Wyatt went to the counter, bought their snacks and drinks, then carried the tray back, setting the contents on the table. He took the seat across from Shy, resisting the urge to sit beside him. That would not be a good idea, he realized.

Besides, he could watch Shy's expressions better this way. Wyatt had a feeling he really needed to pay attention to those. He was feeling his way through unfamiliar territory, and he needed to see Shy's reactions to know when he was keeping to the right path and when he was making a misstep.

He instinctively unscrewed the cap on the water bottle and handed it to Shy.

"Thanks." Shy took it and drank, peering at Wyatt over the bottle. *Such beautiful blue eyes.* Wyatt ached to get them on canvas.

Where to begin? Wyatt wanted to know everything, but what subjects were safe? The last thing he wanted was to make Shy uncomfortable. Or, worst-case scenario, cause him to run.

"Have you lived in the neighborhood long?"

"Fifteen years."

The response surprised Wyatt. And unsettled him. He did the mental math. Assuming Shy to be maybe twenty or twenty-one, that meant… he'd been just a little boy? What the hell. He swallowed his next words, rather than blurt out something harsh about Randy. He needed facts, not conjecture.

"Oh." He kept his voice deliberately noncommittal. "Long time."

Shy nodded. He reached for the bag of popcorn, popped a swollen kernel between his lips with careful deliberation. Wyatt watched, fascinated by the grace in his motion. His cock gave a twitch.

"Where did you and Randy live before that?" Wyatt ripped open his bag of barbecue chips, releasing a spicy fragrance he could fairly taste. Shy's eyes flickered briefly to the chips and away.

"Nowhere." The reply was sharp and succinct. "That's when we moved in with him. Fifteen years ago."

Tread lightly... lightly....

"Hey, I'll trade you some of my chips for some of your popcorn?" Not waiting for an answer, he placed a few of the crisp red treats in his hand and held it out to Shy, counting on instinct and desire to override whatever held him in check. "Go ahead," he encouraged him. *You know you want to....*

A moment passed that felt like a lifetime before Shy's hand shot out and claimed the chips, and he practically inhaled them. After he chewed and swallowed, Shy tentatively licked his lips—whether to savor the flavor or remove a telltale trace of spice, Wyatt couldn't be sure.

Shy stiffened and his cheeks flamed as he cast his eyes down on the table. Wyatt got the feeling he was waiting for something... but what? And then it hit him. Shy expected to be punished for what he'd done. Was Randy that strict about his diet?

Or was there more to the story than met the eye? Surely this wasn't just because of a few grams of polyunsaturated fat?

Shy's lower lip trembled. Wyatt had to resist the urge to brush his thumb over it, to reassure him that everything was all right. How could he when he didn't know what was wrong?

He could barely hear the words that forced themselves out. He had to lean in, in spite of himself.

"Please... don't tell... Randy...."

The agony in Shy's eyes tugged at his heart.

SHY FELT each and every beat of his heart. As though the organ had slowed to an agonizing crawl, each reverberation echoing in his ears.

Don't... tell... Randy....

But they were so good, his taste buds protested.

It won't happen again. It can't happen again.

"I won't," Wyatt promised, and everything fell back into place, the world spun back onto its axis, and Shy remembered how to breathe again.

"So, who else lives with you?" Wyatt asked. He nibbled at his chips, careful not to talk through his food, which Shy appreciated. He could still smell them, and that was okay. He liked the spicy scent and wondered if Wyatt's breath smelled of it, or tasted…. He yanked his mind back to the conversation.

"Who… what? Oh, no one. Just us." He turned quizzical eyes to Wyatt.

"Just you? But you said *we* a minute ago. We moved in fifteen years ago. I assumed—"

"My mother." Shy's voice dropped a decibel or three. His eyes fell to the table.

"I'm sorry." Shy felt the warmth of Wyatt's hand as it encompassed his on the table between them.

"Sorry? For what?"

"I didn't realize… I mean… she died, right?"

"Died? Not that I know of. Actually, I have no idea where she is." He didn't dare look at Wyatt, face the contempt that was undoubtedly written there. Maybe this wasn't such a good idea after all. His stomach churned. He suddenly felt sick. Bile rose up his throat, into his mouth.

He hastily stood, shaking off the hand that tried to cling. "I… I…."

"What's wrong?" The voice sounded concerned, but that was an act, all an act, to lull Shy into a false sense of security.

"I… gotta go…." He knew where the restroom was. He should. He'd been coming to this store long enough. Without a backward glance, he raced toward it, pushed through the door of the small men's room, which was happily unoccupied, and into the first stall, where he heaved the contents of his stomach.

WYATT DIDN'T know what the hell to do. He wanted to run after him, see that Shy was all right. Judging by the speed with which he raced toward the back of the store, he must be sick.

He's a grown man, his inner voice argued. *He doesn't need you to babysit him.*

Doesn't he?

Wyatt drummed his fingers across the Formica tabletop, counting the moments since Shy disappeared. Two minutes, three, four…. At five, he'd go after him, leave the groceries where they were and be damned. Who'd bother them, anyway?

At four and a half minutes, he rose from his seat. At four minutes and forty-five seconds, he scooted out. But before he had a chance to act on his gut instinct, Shy headed toward him. He waited until Shy reached their table and kept waiting until Shy sat before resuming his own seat.

"Are you okay?" he demanded to know, his voice fraught with concern.

Shy nodded. He reached for his water and took several very short sips.

"Yes, I'm fine." His attention was riveted on the water bottle, as if it was the most fascinating object in the world. His voice sounded so… mechanical. So… lifeless. So… hopeless.

What in the hell was going on? Wyatt wanted to ask Shy so many questions about so many things. About Shy's mother. About his relationship with Randy. When did it begin, and what did it consist of? Did Shy love the older man, even though he was an ass? Did Randy love Shy? Did he ever hurt him? Why was he so fucking strict with him?

What happened between them when no one else was around?

But Wyatt didn't have the right to ask him these things and he knew it. And something told him that if he said any of the things he was thinking, he'd push Shy away, and whatever fragile connection they might have forged there would be irretrievably broken.

Shy was like a delicate flower. A pale, delicate blossom that was being allowed to languish in darkness and neglect. Wyatt yearned to bring him into the light. To nurture him and allow him to bloom. To ease his tortured soul.

But he just didn't know how.

"Something I ate," Shy added, and the subject closed between them. At least for now. Wyatt was determined to find a way in later. If he could only figure out how.

"So, I guess you went to high school here?" That seemed a safe topic. The local high school was a good one. Certainly nothing to be ashamed of.

Shy's response wasn't what he expected.

"No." He shook his head. "I'm homeschooled."

By whom? Wyatt didn't dare ask. Was it the now-absent mother? Or perhaps Randy had overseen little Shy's education. And wasn't that a disturbing image? Yet, somehow, Wyatt could imagine him doing it, if for no other reason than to keep control over Shylor.

That seemed to be the crux of the matter. It all came down to control. Randy had it, and he exercised it with an iron fist. And Shy seemed helpless to do other than obey.

"Are you in... do you go to college?" Wyatt wasn't surprised when Shy shook his head.

He started to ask another question, but whatever it was left his mind as soon as a cell phone went off. He knew, without thinking hard, that it wasn't his phone, or his ringtone. His own ringtone was E.S. Posthumus's "Nara." This was something generic and ordinary.

And it was Shylor's phone, apparently.

Shy raised the instrument to his lips. "I'm here."

A moment of silence, followed by, "At the store."

Another moment. "Almost."

A longer pause. "I'll be waiting." And then, "Yes, Sir." He hung up, slid the phone into his pocket, and began to rise.

Yes, Sir? What the fucking hell?

"I HAVE to go." Shy could not meet Wyatt's eyes. Shame burned brightly in his heated cheeks. Randy was coming home for lunch and had told him in no uncertain terms to be there. Which meant he was hungry. Or horny. Or both. And looking for a little afternoon delight from Shylor.

Shy didn't want Wyatt's questions. He wasn't sure he could answer them, or even handle hearing them. He was grateful Randy had detected nothing amiss in his own responses to his questions. If Randy ever suspected that he and Wyatt…. He left the thought unfinished.

Besides, there *was* no him and Wyatt. That was a delusion, nothing more.

A pipe dream. He'd read about pipe dreams once, in a play. *The Iceman Cometh.* Shy enjoyed reading plays. Luckily, Randy didn't object, and he owned an impressive collection of them, along with novels and assorted volumes of nonfiction. Most of it was for show. Randy read little fiction, mostly Tom Clancy or W.E.B. Griffin. Or books on chess. He played the game through email, and had an expensive chess set in his study. Woe betide Shy if he should ever— God forbid—knock a piece off the board, even accidentally.

That had happened only once. Shy had been about ten at the time. He hadn't meant to. He'd simply lost his balance, tripped over his own feet, and fallen into it. But his protests had fallen on deaf ears. Both Randy's and hers. Shy had worn the resulting welts for many days afterward. They were a badge of shame, and a reminder to do better in the future.

"Let me come with you."

Shy finally raised his eyes, panic-stricken at the very idea. His mouth dropped open, but he couldn't seem to speak. Consternation crossed Wyatt's face.

"Just to the checkout," he hastily added. "That's all, that's all."

Shy's relief was palpable. Even so, it wasn't a good idea and he knew it. "I can manage." He always had before.

He moved toward the shopping cart. To his dismay, Wyatt moved in tandem with him. "Noooooo." His command came out as an anguished moan.

"I just want to help," Wyatt tried again.

"You can't help. No one can help. I have to go." He turned resolutely away. This had been a mistake, and he'd known it before he even came. But at least it would be a memory he could hold on to, something to think about at times when reality was too much and he needed mental relief from... things.

"I want to see you again."

Shy's eyes went wide and he turned back to Wyatt. "You don't understand! I can't!"

"Then make me understand," Wyatt challenged him. He reached for Shy, his hand ringing Shy's wrist. Shy looked from Wyatt's grip to the other man's intense gaze.

"I can't," he said dully. "I'm not yours to touch. I'm his." He yanked himself forcefully out of Wyatt's grasp and began to push the cart toward the front of the store as if all the demons of Hell were hot on his heels.

WYATT DIDN'T move. He wanted to. God, how badly he wanted to. But he was afraid he'd only make matters worse, even if he didn't understand what matters there were to make worse. But there was something wrong, something seriously wrong here.

Wyatt was in over his head and he knew it.

Despair filled him as he stared helplessly after Shy's retreating figure until he turned a corner, lost to his sight. Shy needed him, he knew it. But he was deliberately keeping Wyatt at arm's length. Why?

And why did he make himself sound like he was someone's possession? Something to be owned, not loved. What was going on, and how long had it been going on? Wyatt ached to know.

He resisted the impulse to follow Shy to the checkout, afraid he'd push the frail young man over the edge of some awful abyss. Before he made another move, he needed to talk to someone, explain the situation and get another take on it. And he knew just the man to call.

He slid back into the cheap plastic bench seat, pulled out his phone, and punched in Lukas's number.

HALF OF Shy was afraid Wyatt had followed him to the checkout lanes. The other half was afraid he hadn't. He told the second half to shut up. As the checker scanned each item, Shy kept his attention riveted on the terminal in front of him. He punched in the PIN of the card he used for purchases made on Randy's behalf. He gave Randy each receipt so he could tally it against his bank statement. As the checker finished his order, Shy held his breath and turned his head. He scanned the aisles, panning along the length of them. From his vantage point, he could see most everything, but his field of vision didn't extend to the back and he saw no sign of Wyatt. Shy breathed a mixed sigh of relief. He finished his transaction and pushed his cart to the long counter beneath the plate-glass windows that overlooked the parking lot, where he carefully loaded everything into the bags he'd brought from home—Randy's mandate. And something Shy agreed was a good idea. Not that Randy had asked him what he thought.

He forced himself to focus on Randy, on his detailed instructions, what he'd told Shylor to have ready when he got there. Once the groceries were in the car and the cart pushed into the closest corral, he slid into the driver's seat. A twinge of regret pierced his heart, one he could not properly define.

Wyatt would quickly forget him. Shy would just be an odd tale to tell his friends, someone to laugh about. A joke. A nobody.

Shy couldn't stop thinking about Wyatt.

So not good.

Chapter Four

SHY THOUGHT that Randy was a confusing mass of contradictions. He didn't even pretend to understand the man, despite having lived in his home for fifteen years, and in his bed for five. He demanded Shy stick to the healthy diet prescribed for him, yet he was not above indulging when the mood struck. He drank far more than his dietician suspected and worked it off with his trainer.

Shy never questioned, he simply obeyed. To question any command was to invite trouble. That he did not need.

Today was obviously going to be a day of indulgence, although Shy never asked why. He just did as he was told, like the obedient robot he was.

Today Randy's requests required Shy to make extra stops. In and out, no time to think, no time to question why. Shy ignored the Masterson house as he passed it on his way home. He pulled the car around back and schlepped everything inside, careful not to drop the expensive vintage he'd been instructed to pick up. On occasions such as this, since Shy was underage, Randy sent him to a particular liquor store, owned by one of his cronies. The man waited for him in the parking lot and slipped Shy whatever Randy wanted so that no money changed hands and no questions were asked. He'd settle with Randy later for providing this service.

Shy didn't care about that. His main concern was not to lose focus. Thoughts of Wyatt would have to wait, perhaps forever.

Shy busted a gut to make sure the house was cleaned according to specifications. There was actually a printed manual, one that Randy updated when he made new acquisitions. Shy had been doing this so long he no longer needed to refer to the pages, but he kept them handy, as a reminder to live up to Randy's standards.

He hadn't been able to gauge Randy's mood from their brief phone call. Nor did the demands he'd made give Shy any clue as to what to expect. That was not unusual. Randy thought of no one but Randy. No one else deserved or received consideration.

Randy arrived five minutes early. Either traffic had been exceptionally good, or he thought he might catch Shy doing something he shouldn't. Shy was careful that there was nothing to be caught at. Lunch was ready. Two thick and juicy hamburgers, cooked to rare perfection, the same way Randy preferred all his meat. Shy had a recipe that included his own special rub and contained spicy peppers that he chopped and worked into the meat. Randy said the heat of the peppers helped burn calories. Shy accepted what he was told without comment.

The bottle of expensive champagne chilled in the ice bucket. The bedsheets had been lightly spritzed with Randy's favorite scent, a custom-blended aroma that combined musk with citrus, with just a hint of mint.

Shy wore nothing, per Randy's instructions. He'd taken a shower and carefully cleansed every orifice. As Randy bounced through the door, Shy felt a measure of relief—Randy wore a smile. Whatever had prompted this spur-of-the-moment luncheon must be a good thing. That should help.

Randy handed Shy his briefcase and headed up the stairs without a backward glance. Shy obediently trailed him up, into the bedroom. Everything was at the ready. The heavy drapes were closed against the sunlight. Lit tea light candles dotted the room. A handblown pink vase sat on the bedside table, filled with stalks of fresh-cut iris. Beside it were laid out what Randy had requested: lube, cock ring, nipple clamps, paddle. Shy gave no thought to how any of these would be used. His not to reason why....

Shy stood beside the bed, eyes cast to the floor, waiting. It was Randy's habit on such occasions to take every last item from his pocket and lay them neatly across the top of his dresser, everything in its proper place. One time an ill-placed coin had rolled off the edge and Shy had scooped it up. He'd earned a rap on the knuckles for his pains.

Once this ritual had been performed, Randy clapped his hands one time. That was Shy's cue to look up. Randy held out his arms, and Shy helped him off with his jacket first, followed by every other article of clothing he wore. Each piece was carefully laid aside, out of harm's way. A single wrinkle could send Randy into a screaming tizzy.

Shy was surprised to find Randy at half-mast already. And without his Viagra, too. The little blue pill sat by the champagne. Randy had been taking the pill for the past couple of years, to enhance his performance. Especially in the club. Shy suspected neither the trainer nor the dietician knew he partook. He wasn't even sure Randy's physician knew. Surely he was too young to need it. It was more of an ego thing. To hold his own against the younger studs and lord it over the older men.

Shy took the fact that Randy was halfway to hard as another sign that things had gone very well today. Probably the client he'd been talking about, the local beverage company. Shy hoped there would be many clients who produced such a pleasant effect on Randy.

Randy scooped up one of the burgers and bit into it. Juices flowed from the meat as he savored each bite, licking his fingers. When he was done, he demolished the second sandwich with ease. Shy's face was impassive. If he'd expected to receive one of the two hamburgers, he didn't show it, waiting for Randy to be done. He handed him the pill and a glass of the champagne.

Apparently this was to be a celebration for one.

Holding the fluted glass in one hand, Randy popped the pill, washing it down with the expensive vintage. Shy could fairly feel the energy that poured from him, the excitement. No doubt a new client had turned him on so much.

Sure wasn't Shy.

Randy laid the empty glass on the table and swiped at his mouth. "He never knew what hit him!" he crowed. "I stole the Big V right out from under Ken Leiland's nose. Wait till he finds out the account he thought was in the bag went to me!"

Shy watched Randy's excitement growing along with his cock, as the Viagra took hold. He'd looked up how it worked once, curious to know the mechanics. Apparently it had to do with specific arteries that weren't working properly, and the pill, which was targeted to them, opened them up. Uninhibited blood flow led to a hard-on. Also a warning about an erection lasting more than four hours. Though people joked about it, there was a medical reason why that was dangerous, and not a very funny one. Luckily, Randy had never been in that situation.

Shy suspected if he were, he'd blame Shy for his dysfunction.

He was under no illusion that Randy was sharing this particular triumph with him. This wasn't the first time he'd come home for a nooner following a particularly satisfying coup at the office. Randy was in love with the sound of his own voice. He enjoyed bragging, and Shy just happened to be in the room. Nothing more.

He couldn't help but think Wyatt would be more considerate.

Lost in his own thoughts, it took a second for Shy to realize Randy's gloating had stopped. He glanced and found Randy's eyes trained on him, and he fought the rising panic that threatened to overtake him, forcing his face into its usual passivity.

Randy tapped one finger against his closed lips, thoughtfully. Shy had no idea what, if anything, he was thinking. He seldom did.

"Stroke yourself hard," Randy commanded, and Shy instantly obeyed. He palmed his soft cock and brought it to an erect state with practiced ease.

"Put on the cock ring," Randy instructed.

Shy hastened to obey. "Yes, Sir." To an outside observer, Randy's calm face was no cause for alarm. But Shy could see the gray eyes beginning to darken, and his skin crawled at the knowledge. What did he know, or what did he think he knew? He fought to keep his breath even. Reveal nothing, give nothing away.

The cock ring resembled a dog's collar, black leather and studded. It was adjustable. At its loosest it was not too bad, but on some settings it could be brutal. It all depended on Randy's mood. Normally Shy was allowed to keep it looser than not.

He left it in that particular position, awaiting more orders.

"Tighter," Randy instructed.

Shy adjusted it a notch.

"Again."

Shy pulled it as far as it would go, trapping his erection in the viselike grip. It was painful now, but he didn't let on. It wouldn't be forever, just until they were done here.

Randy's expression was inscrutable. Shy had regained control once more. He presented his usual compliant face to the man who considered himself his Master, his Dominant. Dom, for short. Randy had rules, and Shy obeyed them. Randy had begun to instill his rules into Shy at the age of fifteen. After he bought Shy from Shy's mother, Doreen.

Shy knew nothing else. He had been too young to remember a life before Randy. If he'd had a father, he didn't know him, and the man was never spoken of.

Shy waited patiently for Randy's next command. He assumed Randy would wish to be lubed, and would want Shy to prepare himself for his entrance. Although Randy had requested the paddle, Shy didn't anticipate he would use it. That was generally for discipline purposes and seldom used. There were different types of paddles. This one was wooden, and it hurt. But this was the one Randy had specified.

Shy had been paddled a lot in the beginning, when he was just a child. He'd confused the strokes with love. He knew differently now. There was no love between them, only obedience. Love was not real, it was a myth. The subject of sappy books and stupid fairy tales.

Love did not exist.

Randy poured himself another glass of champagne and sipped at it, regarding Shy over the rim. "Have a good day?"

Shy nodded, not trusting his voice. Where had that question come from?

"Anything… *special*… happen?"

"I got what you asked for." As if catering to Randy's every whim were the only special occasions in Shy's life.

The eyes seemed darker, unblinking. Shy fought against the need to run.

Fuck me and go. Please.

"Anything you want to tell me?"

Shy shook his head.

Randy surprised Shy by taking a seat on the edge of the bed, close to the table. Closer to the lube, perhaps?

Randy patted his bare thighs. "Bend over."

Wh-what?

"Now."

Oh Jesus, why hadn't he moved fast enough, when the words first left Randy's lips? Not stopping to think, Shy did as he was told, stretching out across Randy's lap.

Please, don't let him be mad, don't let him be mad, don't let—

The first stroke took Shy by surprise. He released an inadvertent gasp. Randy didn't seem to notice or care. The hard wood bit into Shy's tender flesh. It stung. The next one felt a little harder. So were the third and fourth.

Pain flamed through his body like wildfire, a liquid warmth that stole through his veins. He gritted his teeth, knowing Randy couldn't see, not with his head bent as it was.

When Randy paused, Shy prayed that he was done. That he'd order him onto the bed and then fuck him. The bottle of champagne clunked on the table. Must have wanted another drink.

The cold, wet liquid shocked Shy. It burned into his bruised cheeks and stung like the very devil. This time he couldn't help the moan. It was wrung from him, against his will.

He felt Randy's tongue lap at his wet skin. It didn't ameliorate the pain in any way.

Tears stung his eyes.

"You're mine, Shylor. No one else's," Randy hissed.

Oh fuck….

The sting of the alcohol permeated Shy's skin, sending sharp sensations cascading through him. Just as those started to blessedly dull, Randy brought the paddle down again… and again…. Fresh waves assaulted Shy. His nether cheeks flamed, seared with a heat that refused to quit.

When he was younger and Randy had spanked him, Shy used to squirm on Randy's lap, trying to escape the pain. He'd learned quickly enough not to do that. It only made things worse. He lay still now.

"Who do you belong to?" Randy demanded to know, striking a fresh blow.

"You," Shy mumbled automatically, his response muffled against Randy's thigh.

"I can't hear you!"

Shy lifted his head slightly, just enough to make himself heard. "You. Only you, Sir." No need to think, just spit it out. Nothing less would do.

When Randy made no immediate reply, Shy thought the worst was over. Until he felt Randy's teeth press against his inflamed skin. *Oh please no, not now, please not now....* Shy's inner plea a mantra of protection against what he feared Randy might do.

But it didn't help. He could feel Randy's teeth pierce his flesh, and a searing pain went through him. This was not the first time Randy had bitten him, whether in anger or lust. Sitting would be a bitch tomorrow, and Shy knew it.

At times like these, Shy absented himself, separated his mind from his body and did his best to not feel the pain. Nonsense phrases and silly songs played themselves in his mind. Monkeys and weasels raced one another round and round the mulberry bush. London Bridge fell down and dreams flew over the rainbow.

The paddle fell once, twice more, before Randy mercifully stopped what he was doing. At least that aspect of it.

"You will *not*... ruin... my mood. D'you hear me?"

"Yes, Sir." Shy made sure to make himself heard this time, trying to focus on anything but the throbbing in his ass.

"So red," Randy crooned, as if he'd actually accomplished something he was proud of. "Like a cherry. Like the cherry I took. Remember?"

How could Shy forget?

Shy's cheeks were pulled apart, and then Randy jammed something inside without warning. Felt like his thumb, maybe. Shy gasped at the intrusion.

"So fucking tight. Perfect fit for me, and *no one* else."

Shy's protesting muscles opened, forced to relax at the intrusion.

"Damn straight I'm gonna fuck you."

Suddenly, Shy felt empty. Randy had withdrawn his thumb. He slapped Shy's ass, producing a wince.

"Get on the bed," he commanded. "Quickly. I can't stay here all day. Have to get back to work."

"Yes, Sir." Shy scrambled to obey, although his rubbery legs protested. For a moment, he worried he'd fall to the floor, incurring Randy's further wrath. But they held, just long enough for him to flop on the bed and assume the position, ass invitingly in the air. No matter that it hurt like a son of a bitch.

Please just let this end....

He couldn't see what was happening, but the bed quivered as Randy put his weight on it. Shy tried to return to the other place, the safe place, but his mind wouldn't cooperate, filled with images he could not shake loose. He didn't want to think about what was going to happen, but he couldn't stop, and he tensed up, his arms stiffening, his body clenching, as if to prevent Randy's entrance.

No, no. It'll hurt more....

Randy came in behind him, moving into position for the kill. He wished he knew how to pray, but his mother had never taken him to church. Told him there were cocksucking perverts there.

Watch out for the cocksuckers, boy....

Somewhere along the line, she'd managed to change her mind about those, at least when it came to Randy Grant. Didn't stop her from selling her only child to one of the alleged perverts. Obviously money talked, and it talked loudly. Loud enough to cover a multitude of sins.

"Is something wrong?"

Wyatt's words came tumbling into Shy's mind. He could see Wyatt standing there, his shadow falling over Randy's expensive sedan, a white knight minus the steed.

Shy knew better, but he couldn't help himself. Wyatt filled his brain to the exclusion of all else, as if Shy'd lapsed into a dreamlike state from which he might never emerge. He pictured Wyatt behind him, imagined his beautiful cock sliding in and out of Shy, filling him with the greatest pleasure. Wyatt wasn't too big and he wasn't too little—he was just right. And he knew just what to do, the right way to move, drawing his own pleasure from Shy's eager body.

Take me, Wyatt, I'm yours....

He relaxed into Wyatt's masterful touch, which overrode the pain, even as Shy rose above it, floating on the strength of his own dreams. Never mind that his cock was swollen and angry, leaking precome but unable to find release because of the leather ring. Never mind any of it, just keep on dreaming....

He was shaken from his torpor by the grunts of Randy's orgasm. Randy pulled out just before he collapsed onto the bed, one arm flung over his eyes as he worked at catching his breath.

Shy's eyes widened as he realized what he'd just done, and he was barely able to keep himself from trembling. He watched Randy, fearful of what he'd do if he realized, if he sensed Shy's illicit fantasy. Maybe this time he'd go over the edge and... he couldn't complete the thought even to himself.

"Shylor...." Randy panted, and Shy held his breath. This was it. "Go get a washcloth and clean me up. Make sure it's warm." And that was all. Apparently Randy hadn't noticed.

Shy almost peed himself in his gratitude at not being caught.

He hurried to the bathroom, ignoring the pain that radiated through his limbs, especially his ass where Randy had bitten him, wet the cloth, and brought it back to cleanse Randy. When he was done, Randy got up and dressed, his usual smirk fixed firmly in place.

"Don't take that off." He pointed to the cock ring. "And clean yourself up."

What did this portend?

"We're going to the club tonight, my little slave."

CHAPTER FIVE

WYATT LINGERED for a few minutes after Shy had gone, in the vain hope that he'd return. That maybe they'd pick up the pieces of their shattered time together… and maybe Wyatt could help put the pieces in place, help make Shy whole.

But he was fooling himself and he knew it. The little he'd heard of Shy's conversation told him a different story. Shy's eerie *"Yes, Sir"* still echoed in his head…. He knew there was no coming back.

Lukas didn't ask unnecessary questions, luckily. He agreed to meet Wyatt at the house in about an hour and told Wyatt to chill until he arrived. That would give time for Wyatt to put his thoughts in order. What was he going to say? That he thought it was creepy that Shy called Randy *Sir*?

And when asked, what reason could he give for even caring?

When he pulled Masterson's big luxury car into the drive, he glanced across the street. No sign of Randy. He parked and went inside, still debating what he was going to say. By the time Lukas showed up, approximately an hour after they'd spoken, he'd yet to think of anything.

He opened the door to his mentor, forcing a cheerfulness into his voice that he was far from feeling. "Enter at your own risk," he intoned in the accents of an Eastern European bloodsucker. Rather than laughing, Lukas cocked an eyebrow at him and handed him the paper bag he held.

"What's that?" Wyatt stared at it as if he'd never seen one before.

"Cheap wine. Sometimes you just have to do it." Lukas brushed past him, more familiar with the house than Wyatt. "I'll grab the glasses and meet you in the living room." His voice brooked no argument, and Wyatt had none to give.

Tossing the bag into a trash can, Wyatt set the bottle on the glass-topped coffee table, slumping onto the white brocade sofa. Lukas joined him moments later, stemware in his hand. He set it down and poured. Neither spoke as Wyatt studied his mentor, still debating what he would say now that he was there.

Lukas Callahan was a respected artist in his own right. Wyatt had been lucky to catch his eye at the university, at a student art show. Lukas had taken Wyatt under his wing—he was his mentor as well as his friend. In his early forties, Lukas took good care of himself. His hair was pure black, without a trace of gray. His brown eyes were warm cups of coffee against his tan skin. A well-manicured goatee surrounded pale red lips.

And right now, his eyes seemed to bore into Wyatt's very soul, which didn't help.

Lukas handed him a glass of wine. He took the other and seated himself beside Wyatt, leaning back, one arm across the back of the couch as he sipped, staring at Wyatt over the rim.

"How's your art coming?"

"Fine, just fine." Wyatt twiddled with the stem of the glass, looking away from Lukas. Somehow he knew that wouldn't fly.

"So, let me guess. If it's not your work, then it's a man that's troubling you?"

Damn, Lukas knew him too well, didn't he?

Wyatt nodded.

"You going to tell me or make me play Twenty Questions?"

Wyatt looked up. Of course he wanted to talk, but somehow the words weren't coming.

"What do you know about that guy across the street?" he blurted out.

Lukas paused, glass halfway to his lips. His eyes narrowed slightly. "Since the Talbots aren't there, I assume you're talking about Randy Grant?"

Wyatt nodded again.

Lukas stared for another moment, his eyes piercing and far too intuitive for Wyatt's own good. "Oh shit," he mumbled, draining the glass and reaching for the bottle. "Wyatt, what have you done?"

Wyatt frowned. "I haven't done anything, what do you mean?"

"When I suggested you watch John's house, I didn't think you'd run out and try to make friends with the neighbors. What have you been doing?"

"I met them. That's all," Wyatt replied defensively.

"Them? Oh double shit."

Wyatt felt a flush rise up his cheeks. He hid his discomfort by drinking more of the cheap wine. The taste was growing on him as its warmth stole through his veins.

"If I thought for even one minute you'd want anything to do with Grant—"

"I don't want anything to do with *him*," Wyatt interrupted.

"That's what I was afraid of." Lukas groaned. "I told myself that Randy'd never be your cup of tea. Shylor, on the other hand...."

"What is their relationship, Lukas? Do you know? You sound like you know them, right?" Wyatt didn't realize he clutched the glass too tightly until Lukas peeled it from his fingers and set it down on the table.

"I know too much." He sighed. "Yes, I know them. I've known them for years. I remember when Randy first moved in. That must be twenty years ago, something like that."

"Is he a friend?"

Lukas snorted. "Hardly. The only friend that man has is himself."

"So you've known Shy for a long time too?"

Lukas groaned again. "Shy, is it? And just how did you become acquainted with him? I bet that couldn't have been easy."

"Well, I saw him washing the car one day, and I just walked across the street and said hello."

"I bet Randy just loved that."

Wyatt noticed Lukas never asked if Randy knew, as if that was a given. "Not really."

"Not surprised." He inched forward on the sofa, looked earnestly into Wyatt's eyes. "Is he the reason you called me?"

"Yeah." Wyatt licked his suddenly dry lips, visions of Shy filling his head. His heart ached inexplicably, and he attempted to drown it, pouring more of the cut-rate brew.

"Wyatt," Lukas began slowly, as if measuring his words carefully. "You have no idea what's going on there, and I don't think you want to know."

"Yes, I do," Wyatt whispered. "Please, Lukas."

A long moment of silence. Lukas sighed. "Very well."

Lukas didn't speak immediately. He poured himself more wine and drained the glass, then replaced it on the coffee table. He repositioned himself in the corner of the sofa, one leg crooked across the cushions, the other maintaining a position on the floor.

Wyatt held his tongue, half dreading the words he might hear. A sour anticipation held sway in the pit of his stomach. He was afraid to add to it with any more wine. He watched Lukas's left hand carefully. That was the tell to what he was thinking or feeling. He rubbed his thumb against each of the digits in turn in a constant motion.

That movement was an indicator of uncertainty on Lukas' part. The feeling grew stronger as Wyatt rose and paced across the room, pulling back the blinds to gaze across the street. The sedan was there now. He dropped the curtains into place, returned to the sofa, and fell heavily onto it, his attention riveted on Lukas.

"I'm just not sure where to begin," Lukas confessed. "This isn't a conversation I ever thought we'd need to have, to be honest."

"How about starting with Randy and Shy? What's their relationship?" Wyatt leaned toward his mentor, as if proximity would ease the severity of whatever needed to be said. Maybe he was wrong, maybe he'd read something into them that didn't exist. "Is Randy his father?" That would explain the *Sir*, but not the kiss.

At the look in Lukas's eyes, Wyatt's heart sank.

"Hardly."

Another long pause. Wyatt reached for the wine bottle, upended the remains into his glass, then chugged them. Damn his stomach anyway.

"Shylor and Doreen moved in when Shy was just a little kid. Maybe fifteen years ago. Something like that. She was Randy's housekeeper."

Wyatt tapped an impatient foot into the carpet. There had to be more than that.

"About five years ago, Doreen left and Shy stayed."

"Why did she leave? Why did Shy stay? That doesn't answer my question, Lukas. What's their relationship?"

"I think you already have some idea about that." Lukas looked him square in the eyes. Wyatt found he couldn't pretend any more.

"They're a couple?"

"I'm not sure that's the word I'd use," Lukas cautiously replied.

"But they're together, right? That old goat is fucking a kid young enough to be his son?" Wyatt felt incensed on Shy's behalf. And frustrated. And thoroughly disgusted.

Lukas held up one hand. "Just putting this out there, but that 'old goat' is my age, Wyatt. You want to rephrase that?"

"Sorry, I didn't mean anything, you know that…." Wyatt forced himself to take a deep, calming breath. "But he's still a hell of a lot older than Shy. And five years ago? What was Shy then? Fifteen? Sixteen? That has to be illegal."

"Probably, but who's going to press charges? Shy's mother's not here. Shy? Hardly."

"But… but… but…." Wyatt sputtered ineffectually, trying to grasp the concept that Randy Grant had taken a young boy into his bed… an undoubtedly innocent young boy… and was holding him hostage there to this very day.

He replayed the scene in the grocery store for the millionth time in his head.

"He called him *Sir*." Wyatt's voice was barely audible.

"What?"

"When we were together, he called him *Sir*. On the phone."

"Shit, Wyatt."

"I know, that's creepy, right?"

"No, not shit for that. Shit because you and him… you were together? Where? How?"

"He met me at Shop for Less. Today. Then the Keeper called and he said he had to go. Called him *Sir*."

"The what?"

"The Keeper. That's what I call Randy."

Lukas rolled his eyes. "Can't say I'm surprised, though. Did he know about you?"

"Grant? No, I don't think so."

"Good. Nothing else matters." Lukas breathed a sigh of obvious relief. "Tell you what, Wy, go into the liquor cabinet and bring out a bottle of something stronger. We're going to need it, I think. I'll square it with John later. That won't be a problem."

"Like what?"

"Some of his expensive bourbon. The black label."

Wyatt wasted no time in doing as Lukas asked, going into the private stock of liquor in the study. He brought back the nearly full bottle of Masterson's finest bourbon and two clean glasses. He pushed the empty wine bottle and fluted glasses to the side. He'd pick them up later.

"Here, let me." Lukas took the bottle from him. Wyatt hadn't realized until that moment that his hands were shaking. Lukas poured three good fingers in each glass, handed one to Wyatt.

"Sip it," he advised. "Slowly."

Though Wyatt wanted to bolt it as fast as he could, he obeyed.

"Okay, now listen to me, Wyatt. Are you listening?"

Wyatt nodded, not trusting his voice.

"There's a whole lot more to this than just them sleeping together."

"Do you think… Grant loves him?"

Lukas groaned. "Damn, Wyatt, that's such a tough call to make."

"Is it? You said you know them. You've seen them together. What do you think?"

"I think it's complicated. But just between us, no, not in any normal sense of the word. Keep sipping." He indicated the smoky liquid in Wyatt's glass. "It's going to get worse before it gets better."

I can do this. I can. If Shy can live through this… whatever this is… surely I can just listen to whatever it is….

"When I was very young, I met a man named Bobby Demaris. He took a liking to me, and he became my mentor."

Wyatt wrinkled his brow in perplexity. "I don't know any artist by that name."

"No, he's not an artist. At least not in the sense that you mean."

"Then how did he mentor you?"

"Bobby has a club, a very special club. It's a private club, in West County. Bobby D's Sweet Majesty is the full name, but most of the members just call it Sweet Majesty for short."

"Okay, so he has a club." Wyatt was still confused, but at a look from Lukas, he stilled his tongue.

"This has nothing to do with art, and everything to do with obedience. With pleasure and pain. With domination and submission."

Wyatt couldn't seem to help himself, the words just rolled off his tongue. "What are you telling me? You're a disciple of the Marquis de Sade?" He snorted his amusement, even if the joke was ill-timed and in questionable taste. But when Lukas didn't laugh, Wyatt quieted immediately. "Oh fuck…."

"Very eloquent, even if oversimplified. Just rid yourself of any lurid images that are flashing through your mind. And forget about all those B movies with whips and chains and torture chambers…."

Wyatt breathed a sigh of relief. "So none of that exists?"

"Oh yes, it does. Very much so. But the reality isn't what you think it is. And you'd be surprised at who all practices it."

A pulse point at Wyatt's temple began to pound.

"Keep sipping," Lukas advised.

He raised the glass to his lips, allowing the amber liquid to burn its way down his throat.

"B-D-S-M." Lukas checked each letter off on a finger. "*B* is for bondage, *d* is for discipline. It's also for dominance. *S* is for submission, and *m* masochism. But there's variations. Bondage and discipline. Dominance and submission. Sadism and masochism. BDSM has become sort of catchall phrase for a lot of activities under one umbrella. But however you spell it, or whatever letters or words you use, what it comes down to is a way of life. One that many people take very seriously."

Wyatt's head was spinning with the overabundance of information. "How do you know so much about this…." His words trailed off as his brain caught up with the conversation. "So you… you're into this? And this club you're talking about…?"

"Yes, I am, and Sweet Majesty is where I go to meet with like-minded individuals. People with the same sorts of… interests."

That was a whole lot to take in at one time. "What goes on there?" He was almost afraid to know. "People walking around in leather? Or nude? Orgies? Spankings, beatings… what? And what do you do? I mean, what do you call yourself? I mean…." He noticed a slight tinge of red color Lukas's cheeks.

"I call myself your friend is what I call myself." He took a deep breath and regained his normal coloring. "I know this is a lot," he agreed, "but you wanted to know. I'm what you would refer to as a Dom. A Dominant. But it's a lot more than just telling someone what to do. It's developing a level of trust with your submissive, and it's learning about his needs and understanding them and taking care of them and him."

A terrible suspicion grew in Wyatt's breast, one he was afraid to put voice to. And yet, how could he do otherwise?

He took a long sip of the bourbon, desperately seeking answers in its warmth. But none was forthcoming from that source. Lukas was the only one who had those. "What has this got to do with…. I mean, all this stuff about that club. And about BDSM. Where does Shy come into this? Shy and Randy, I guess? I'm not following." If he understood correctly, these things happened years ago, long before Shy was even born.

Did he really want to know the truth?

Wyatt drew a deep breath, tightened his grip on the glass, and forced himself to listen.

"I knew Randy before he moved into the neighborhood," Lukas confessed. "I was the one who told him the house was for sale. Even though he was young, he was already a successful businessman. Plus his family had some money. Enough for him to buy the house."

"Did you meet him at— Is he a member of… your club?"

Lukas nodded. "He is."

"And… is he a Dom, did you say? Like you?"

There was a long pause. So long that Wyatt thought Lukas didn't intend to answer. But finally, Lukas shifted his position on the couch again and replied. "He considers himself a Dom, but from what I've seen of them, I think it's more of a Master/slave relationship. He… he has no idea of what it really means to be a Dom. It's men like him that give the lifestyle a bad name. All he wants is control, that's all. He gives no real thought to Shy's well-being."

"Oh dear God." Wyatt was appalled. His hand shook so badly he had to set the glass onto the coffee table. "Does he… does he take Shy… there?"

Lukas nodded. "Sometimes. Sometimes he comes alone. Wyatt, are you sure you want to hear more?"

A tight band had formed about Wyatt's heart, squeezing mercilessly. "Yes," he replied, his voice almost a growl. "I need to know, Lukas. Tell me."

Lukas swallowed hard, his eyes meeting Wyatt's. "He parades Shy in front of the others as his possession. Sometimes naked. Often naked. Often at the end of a chain. He does it to show off his virility. It's an ego thing." Lukas's voice held a measure of disgust that he couldn't hide. "He… he tells him what to do, and Shy does it. No matter what."

"Such as?" Wyatt clenched his fists, a rage such as he'd never felt before growing inside his chest, threatening to tear him apart if he heard any more.

"Such as servicing anyone Randy tells him to. Oral only," Lukas hastily added. "No one is allowed… that is, he doesn't have to…."

"So the great Randy doesn't allow anyone to fuck Shy? How kind of him."

"Kindness has nothing to do with it, I'm afraid," Lukas said. "No one touches what's Randy's without his permission. No one."

SHY SHIVERED, although the night was far from cold. Cloyingly humid even after the sun had gone down, there was a thick type of St. Louis heat that made breathing difficult. Still, Shy shivered, clutching his coat tighter about him as he climbed into Randy's sedan.

The first time Randy had taken Shy to Sweet Majesty, Shy had been deep in the throes of what he thought was love. Excited to be going out and proud to be seen with Randy. He'd been too young and too naïve to know enough to be scared of what might happen. This was before he'd learned that love did not exist, not for guys like him. Now he knew the truth, and he numbed himself to everything around him.

At least that's what he told himself, in order to get through another night at the club.

The cock ring was painful, but it was endurable. What Shy hated most was leaving the house in a long black coat, wearing nothing underneath. He felt entirely exposed, although he realized no one who saw him could possibly know his shame. Randy dressed to the nines for such occasions, more than happy to show off his designer wardrobe. He'd undress once they arrived, and only if it suited his fancy. Shy didn't have the same luxury.

At least Randy waited until they were inside the club to add his final touch in the form of a black studded collar, attached to a long black leather leash.

The club sat in isolated splendor on top of a large hill. Apparently the owner possessed a lot of acreage. There were no near neighbors. Probably just as well. Cut down on complaints to the police department. Although from what Shy had observed, some of the club's clientele belonged to the legal profession and would probably quash any trouble should it arise.

Large fluted columns supported the two-story building. Shy had heard Randy refer to it as being antebellum, once belonging to a man who owned slaves. Fitting. It still held slaves, just a different kind.

An impenetrable perimeter of trees ringed the grounds nearest the house, making unwanted observation impossible. Sometimes, in the right weather, scenes were played outside. There was an intricately maintained maze that saw more than its share of action. And small, secluded cabins for the use of privileged guests who wished to stay longer.

Apparently Randy did not rate access to the cabins for, to his knowledge, Randy had never stayed in one of them. He was sure Randy would have bragged about the experience, if he had.

Randy had not gone back to work after his celebratory fuck, but neither had he spent the time idly. He'd stayed in his home office, conducting business—at least that was Shy's assumption—freeing Shy to attend to his daily chores in peace. He'd even taken his dinner there, saving Shy the trouble of shielding his thoughts from him across the dinner table. Although that also made Shy wonder what he intended to do at the club if he didn't plan to eat, since a night at Sweet Majesty generally involved a meal. Obviously not tonight.

Shy had barely eaten, his appetite having deserted him. After Randy had finished and come out of his office, Shy attended him in the shower and then laid out his clothes for him—a pearl-gray pinstripe suit, white button-down shirt with silver threads running through it, a gray-green textured tie. Shy handed him each article of clothing as it was required.

They were met at the door of the club by the most discreet of men. His name was Mel and he was the butler, the valet, the soul of discretion, and so much more. Garbed in crisp black tails and immaculate white gloves, he was tall and thin and balding, and wore his own innate arrogance, that was reflected in the manner in which he distinguished between his treatment of the guests and that of their companions. When Randy removed Shy's sheltering coat, Mel took it and wished Randy a good evening, leaving them to wander through the house as they would.

Shy stood perfectly still as Randy attached the collar and leash. Randy was in unusually high spirits, his face flush with excitement. Shy couldn't help but notice the very visible outline of Randy's cock in his tightly cut trousers. He wondered if Randy planned to use that tonight. Perhaps it would serve to keep himself from the limelight, which he hated.

Or it could bring him directly into it. Not like he had a choice.

Whenever Randy chose to bring Shy with him, they seemed to draw a small crowd of admirers. Most of them were relegated to the category of do-not-touch-the-merchandise. But there were a favored few who were allowed small favors, beneath Randy's watchful eye. They fondled Shy's cock and pinched his nipples and congratulated Randy on having such a fine specimen, as if Shy were a horse they were interested in purchasing for breeding purposes. In this case, though, Shy played the part of the dam, and not the sire. It was a twisted comparison at best.

First came the obligatory parade through the various rooms of the club. The public ones, that was. The private ones were not to be troubled by anyone, and remained closed to view. But there was more than enough activity in the rooms that were accessible to make up for that. It seemed that most of Sweet Majesty's members were very willing to be seen, as well as to see.

Shy hated the eyes that devoured him whole. Hungry eyes and lewd lips that licked and promised and laughed and leered. They didn't see him, they saw his body… and they wanted him. Some were familiar faces, regulars who spent too much of their lives in this club. Others were simply there for business purposes. They all seemed to be connected, in one way or another. Shylor didn't care, and he didn't bother to memorize their names or their occupations. It was their faces he wished to forget. The touch of their hands on his cock. Tonight, his painfully hard cock.

He'd had no relief, unlike Randy.

But he had no choice in the matter. He was forced to endure. So he absented himself, hid as deeply inside as he could go, ignoring them all, as he usually did.

Tonight, though, there was a difference, something that made this occasion almost palatable.

Tonight, visions of Wyatt danced in his head, and they kept him sane.

Shy was not the only male sporting a collar and leash. Nor was he the only one naked. However, that didn't exactly ameliorate the situation for him. Not that he'd ever say anything. He wouldn't dream of it.

He'd seen enough of Sweet Majesty to have some understanding of its clientele. There were regulars, some of whom were in committed relationships, while others came to meet up with like-minded individuals in order to scratch an itch. And then there were those, such as Randy, who liked to show off what they owned.

Shy was there as Randy's personal property, and he knew it. At one time, he'd been proud of what he was. He knew better now, and was simply resigned to the way things were.

Some of the public rooms had no doors. They'd been removed for voyeuristic purposes. Anything and everything was possible. The club's motto could have easily been *anything goes*.

Tables were interspersed throughout the house, including the hallways. Guests were free to dine wherever they wished. There were at least two stages, for those inclined to perform. Their presence didn't prevent impromptu performances from being held in other areas. Shy had noticed peepholes in some of the rooms, perhaps for those who were shyer about watching. Most simply stared at anything they wished to see.

Other Doms walked their subs on leashes of chain and leather, and some of these latter also wore cock rings, like Shy. Shy was not allowed to speak to any of them, and he only spoke to Randy with permission. Randy, of course, was free to converse with whomever he wished, and he did, for many of these men were his business acquaintances. It was not unusual for Randy to finagle contracts here, using Shy's mouth to seal the deal. Shy couldn't remember the number of blowjobs he'd given at Randy's direction, and he didn't really want to know.

As they passed, Shy noticed an active threesome upon one of the stages. A sub was sandwiched between two Doms, being fucked from either end. At a nearby table, another Dom enjoyed his meal while his sub ate food from a plate set on the floor. This was common practice at Sweet Majesty. Randy never permitted Shy to sit at his level.

In another room, one slave faced the wall, spread-eagled, his hands held in manacles screwed into the wall while his Master worked him over with a whip. Another was bent over a table, his ass high in the air, the flesh striped in crisscross welts from the flogger in his Master's hand.

Shy never knew what to expect when they came here. Sometimes Randy would simply watch the activities of the others. Other times, he wanted to show off his prowess as a cocksman, and would fuck Shy hard. Shy's youth was a coup for Randy, one he wore proudly. Shy didn't exist as a person, and no one knew his name. Here he was simply Randy's possession.

Perhaps tonight would be a look-but-don't-touch night. Randy had made no effort to remove his clothes. Shy couldn't help but notice he was still hard. Sometimes he wished Randy would simply fuck someone else, but that never happened. It no longer mattered to Shy if people watched them fuck. He was used to it. It had long ago ceased to be anything but a perfunctory act, at least on his part.

There were at least three house slaves who circulated about the club, under the direction of Mel, with drink-laden trays. If a patron didn't like what was being offered, he simply had to ask for something else. One passed by them now, dressed only in a thong and a red collar that read Sweet Majesty.

"Good evening, Master Grant, good to see you," the young man greeted Randy.

Shy had stopped when Randy did, at a sharp tug on the leash, and partially turned toward him. Randy took a glass of what might have been champagne, his gaze flicking over the well-hung server.

"I can tell you think so," he riposted, eliciting a practiced smile from the other before he passed along his way. Shy quickly glanced at the floor, his expression revealing nothing.

Randy pulled on the leash and Shy knew, without being told, he was to move again. Up a set of stairs now, to the second floor. Some of these doors were closed, but not soundproof, and snippets of sensuality could be heard as they passed by. Moans and cries of pleasure. "Harder!" "Yes, Sir!" and "Fuck me, please!"

Men passed them going the other way. Some paused to exchange greetings with Randy. Each time Randy tugged on the leash, and Shy halted and waited his next command, like a horse on a bridle.

"This your sub?" one man asked, and Randy quickly replied, "Yes."

"Nice job." Envy laced the voice. "May I?"

"Be my guest," Randy assented smoothly.

Strange hands cupped Shy's balls and stroked his cock. Not for the first time, probably not the last. But no one was foolish enough to venture to touch Shy's ass. The one time someone had come close, Randy had roughly knocked his hand away and yelled, "Mine!" in no uncertain terms.

That had also been the last time.

Shy stood without moving or reacting. He was used to this. Nothing fazed him, he felt nothing. This too would pass.

What if he *touched you... what if those were Wyatt's hands groping your balls? Your cock? What then?*

Where had that come from? Shy startled, accidentally shifting his weight.

Dear God, please don't let Randy....

"What?" Randy's voice held an edge. The fondler had already moved away. Shy stood in frozen horror, wondering what response to make. He wasn't even sure what the question was.

"Shylor!" Randy barked.

Shy knew what that meant. He raised unwilling eyes to Randy's face. "What the fuck—" Randy began.

Shy swallowed hard and took a deep breath. But before he could release a single word, another voice intruded, calling Randy's name, and Randy turned away in obvious annoyance. But only at first.

"Well hello, Ken."

Shy breathed again.

"Hello yourself, Randy. Didn't expect to find you here tonight."

"I could say the same for you, Ken." Randy's voice was clearly laced with pride. Shy knew without being told that this was the man he'd beaten to win his new account, the reason for today's celebration. Shy kept his eyes cast down. It wouldn't do to seem to be listening, even though he was standing right there. "Glad to see you can bounce back from disappointment so well."

"Disappointment?" The confusion in Ken's voice was apparent. Shy instinctively knew that Randy was about to tell the other man the sad bad news, as Randy would say, and was taking great delight in doing so.

"At losing such a prestigious account. But cheer up, there'll be others. Maybe I'll be nice and let you have the next one."

Shy darted a quick glance up, then back to his feet. He'd seen enough. Ken's face was purpling. Shy watched the expensive shoes of both men as Ken took a step toward Randy, who never moved.

"*Let* me?" The querulous voice was rising in pitch and volume, drawing the attention of others. Shy almost shifted his weight, uncomfortably, but thought better of it. "Just who do you think you are, Grant? God's gift to marketing?"

"Well, if the shoe fits," Randy modestly replied.

Shy braced himself for a punch that never came, knowing that if this Ken managed to knock Randy from his feet, Shy would go down too, connected as they were. A silky voice, instead, inserted itself, and a quick peek ascertained that it belonged to Mel. He held one gloved hand to his lips, as if shushing two rowdy children.

"Gentlemen, there will be no fighting. No exception. Mr. Demaris's rules will be followed at all times, is that understood?"

"Of course, of course." Randy's voice never faltered, never lost its equanimity. His words were echoed a moment later by a more disgruntled Ken.

"Perfectly understood."

A snap of the fingers and another server appeared, bearing liquid refreshment. Glasses clinked as they were taken in hand.

"Ken, I do apologize for my thoughtless words. Tonight is not a night for quarreling, but for celebration. Is there some way in which we can bury the hatchet between us?"

Did no one else hear the insincerity that laced Randy's words? Probably not. No one knew him as well as Shy did. Although Shy wasn't sure how well he knew Randy Grant himself.

"They say that to the victor belongs the spoils, don't they? Maybe in this case, the victor should share the spoils?"

Shy pondered this question, waiting for Randy's next scathing remark. It didn't come.

"What did you have in mind, my dear Ken?"

Startled, Shy glanced up again. Mel and the server had gone, leaving them to face one another down, having given them their only warnings. Shy had seen other men removed for such offenses. Violence was not tolerated at Sweet Majesty. At least not that kind. Only the sort inflicted by designated instruments of… delight.

"You have quite the asset there, Randy old boy…."

Randy's flinch traveled through the leash. He hated to have anyone refer to his age. He was very sensitive about it, despite the fact there were men here who were easily forty years his senior.

Suddenly Shy understood Ken's allusion, and his cheeks flamed as he quickly stared at his feet. He desperately fought to control his breathing, his longtime training standing him in good stead.

What was Ken asking for? And would Randy allow it, whatever it was? Not that Shy had any choice in the matter. He'd do what he was told to do, no more, no less.

"I do." Shy couldn't decipher Randy's tone, couldn't tell his mood from those two words alone.

"Maybe you could… share your good fortune with those of us who are… less fortunate?"

Surely he wasn't suggesting…. Shy knew without looking that Randy would never go for that. He had a cardinal rule, and it was never to be broken. No one, but no one, other than himself, was to touch Shylor's ass. Shy had long ago rid himself of the idea that the compulsion was romantic. It was actually very selfish and very self-serving on Randy's part.

Randy would not go where someone else had been. And Randy was scared to death of AIDS.

But if Randy blatantly rejected Ken's suggestion, would the already volatile Ken fly off the handle and get them all bounced out of the club? Perhaps for good?

And would that be such a bad thing?

"Pick a room," Randy said silkily. Randy jerked the leash. Shy knew that meant he should walk behind him, eyes on the ground. He prayed that they were not going into one of the private rooms. If they did, then all would be lost, all bets would be off, and things would get decidedly ugly. Uglier than usual.

Randy flicked the leash again and Shy stopped, taking in his surroundings. To his great relief, it was one of the public rooms, already populated by about six to eight men and four subs. They glanced up as Randy cleared his throat for attention.

"Gentlemen," he began. "Good evening."

Greetings were returned, acknowledgments made. A few seemed interested, some curious, but no one ignored the man who oozed charm and schmooze with every breath. Shy noticed Ken, at Randy's side, seemed equally as captivated as the others and decidedly less hostile.

"I would like," Randy continued, "to share my good fortune with you this evening. Today I made a very profitable business deal with a very special client."

Shy glanced at Ken, who remained silent.

"Therefore, I am giving you all a gift." Curious glances, increased interest now.

Randy indicated Shy with a wave of one well-manicured hand. "Each and every one of you in this room shall receive a blowjob from those pretty lips."

Oh fuck....

Shy squirmed uncomfortably, unable to prevent the shudders that rippled through his body. *Stand still*, he admonished himself. He didn't have permission to move. The last thing he needed was to draw Randy's ire down on him. He was already receiving enough unwanted attention from the rest of the room.

Randy's words were greeted with a moment of silence, as if the other occupants of the room were digesting what he'd said, perhaps considering possibilities. The moment was ended when someone whistled, then someone else catcalled, "He's got some purty lips, hmm-mmmm." That broke the tension as the other men laughed.

This wasn't the first time Randy had offered Shy's services to other members of Sweet Majesty. So why did this time bother him? Was it because the other occasions had been more low-key and private, not this wholesale orgy of lip service he was supposed to pay to virtual strangers?

Shy looked up without thinking, scanning the faces of the men in the room, who all seemed to be staring at him, finally landing on a man somewhere about Randy's age. The man looked distinctly uncomfortable.

"Grant, you're asking an awful lot from him." The man took a step toward Shy. Randy tugged at the leash, jerking Shy, who stumbled to his knees and stayed there.

"He's mine to do with as I please." Randy's voice was smooth on the surface, but Shy felt the undertones of his displeasure. He involuntarily flinched.

Ignoring Randy, the man knelt before Shy, searching his eyes with compassion. "Is this what you want?" he softly asked.

Shy's mouth went dry. Terror flew along every synapse at the thought of what Randy would do should he answer with anything other than *yes*. Yet he seemed unable to get the simple word past his lips. He felt tension on the leash increase. Knew without looking that Randy was staring at him, waiting, anticipating the only response he wanted to hear. The only response Shy dared to give.

And yet he couldn't give it.

Why not? What was wrong with him? Did he want to be hurt? Or worse?

He couldn't say, couldn't do it. So he did the next best thing and nodded, hoping his performance was an Oscar winner, since everything was riding on it.

The man looked unconvinced.

"You heard him," Randy said smoothly, despite the fact that Shy hadn't uttered a single syllable. "Would you like to be first, Blankenship?"

An expression of disgust crossed the man's face. He placed his fingers beneath Shy's chin, tilted his face up. "You don't have to do this," he pled with him.

Before he had a chance to respond, assuming he had any such intention, Randy yanked Shy's leash, and he fell from the man's grasp and onto the floor.

When the man would help him, Randy snarled, "Do. Not. Touch."

Shy scrambled back onto his knees, his face impassive.

Blankenship murmured, "God help you, son," and rose to his feet, facing Randy. "I intend to report you, Grant. You give those of us who are honestly living the life a bad name. You have no idea what being a Dom entails. You're a clueless piece of shit."

"You can't talk to me like that." Randy's usually cultured voice had an edge to it now.

Shy felt the leash tremble. He glanced up in surprise. Randy was rubbing his arm, probably to keep himself from punching the other man.

"I have every right to be here, same as you. Now just mind your own business." Randy turned away, toward a younger man with gelled blue hair and an Armani suit. He'd been one who'd seemed excited at Randy's offer. "Harry, you want to be first? Let Shy show you what he can do with those lips."

"Yeah, sure, Randy." The young man eagerly stepped forward, already unzipping himself. Shy heard more whistles, mixed with angry murmurs. He could barely breathe, barely focus.

Just do what needs to be done, get it over with.

He sniffled once, forced himself to breathe, and willed his body not to shake. If this was Randy's wish, what could he do but obey? What choice did he have?

He sensed bodies in motion around him. A few of the men had left, but others were queuing up behind Mr. Blue Hair, laughing and joking about who would come the most, who would last the longest. Shy felt sickened at their words.

"Grant, for the love of all that's right, stop this." That was Blankenship again. Even as the young man before him pulled his cock from his pants, Shy was able to observe Randy. He couldn't help but watch. The leash jerked almost erratically in Randy's hand as he rubbed at his neck. Shy could fairly see the veins stand out, while Randy's face was flushed with displeasure.

Shy tried to absent himself, move into a distant corner of his mind where none of this existed. Let his body obey, do what it had to, but he wouldn't be there. He'd be far away, in another place entirely. And in this faraway place, Shy was not alone—Wyatt was there, standing with him.

Wyatt....

Shy mentally reached for him, felt the warmth of Wyatt's embrace, as he imagined it to be, even as he felt the blue-haired young man's cock brush over his lips. "Open wide for chunky," the other man joked.

Shy jerked back from the man's touch, his body reacting faster than his brain. *What have I done?* Panic-stricken, he raised fearful eyes to Randy, unsure what Randy would do. He hated disobedience, and he didn't tolerate it. With his actions, Shy had as much as told him no. For that, he'd have to pay a price.

Randy turned furious eyes to Shy. He took a step toward him. Shy quivered. Blankenship moved toward Randy, as if to intercede on Shy's behalf. Shy wanted to warn him not to bother, he'd only make things worse. But then something odd happened. Randy's eyes widened, his mouth gaped open, and his hands released the leash, clawing at his chest instead.

As Shy watched, Randy crumpled before his very eyes, and the room exploded into chaos.

"Call 9-1-1!"

CHAPTER SIX

TIME BEGAN to move in funny ways. Sometimes it was stretched out, like pulling on taffy. Then it seemed that people moved about Shy in slow motion, their words as incomprehensible as if spoken in a foreign tongue. And then sometimes time jerked and pulled, and passed without his being aware of what happened.

He sat in the eye of the storm, his mind devoid of thought. Nothing made sense. Nothing. The cries of "Do something" and "Call 9-1-1!" faded. The only constant was Randy, who lay on the floor, unmoving. So Shy sat where he was, and also didn't move, for he'd not been told he could, so he wouldn't.

By the time the paramedics arrived with the stretcher, someone had dressed Shy in a pair of sweatpants and a T-shirt and removed his collar and his cock ring, freeing his numb cock. But that didn't seem to matter, did it? The pants were too big and the crotch hung to his knees, but he didn't care. His eyes were fixed on Randy, waiting for him to say something. Anything.

But his lips never moved.

Shy watched the paramedics carefully, although what they were actually doing, he couldn't say. None of it made any sense. All of it was gibberish.

But he understood they were taking Randy somewhere else, that much was plain. As was the fact that he needed to go with them. When they loaded Randy onto the stretcher and began to walk him from the room, Shy automatically rose and followed.

"Where are you going?" one of them asked.

"With you." That seemed obvious. At least Shy thought so.

The man shook his head, but he never paused, and Shy simply kept walking after them. He *had* to go. That's what he was meant to do. If he didn't, Randy would be pissed, and he knew it.

Then time jumped and he found himself in a room like an office, with two men. Randy and the paramedics were gone. Shy recognized the man who'd told Randy to leave Shy alone. The other seemed familiar too. It took a moment, but Shy realized he was the owner of the club. Shy sat on a small couch. The two men sat in chairs by the desk.

"I know he wanted to go along, but that just wasn't possible," Blankenship was saying.

"I know, I know." Bobby—that's his name, Shy remembered— ran a hand through his close-cropped gray hair. "Damn, what a mess."

"He brought it on himself."

"Yeah, I know that too."

"We have to do something about...."

Shy raised his head. Him? Were they talking about him? Must be. They were both looking directly at him.

"Has he got family?" Blankenship wanted to know.

"Only Grant, God help him."

They fell silent, while Shy's mind kicked around the idea of family for a few seconds but came up empty. The concept was too alien for him to dwell on. Doreen didn't count. She'd never wanted him and told him so often enough. Told him never to call her *mother*. So he hadn't—she'd beaten the word out of him.

Shy replayed the scene again, saw Randy fall to the ground, watched the escalating panic, as though he was watching a video. It still made no sense. When would they take him to Randy? He should be there when Randy woke, or there'd be hell to pay.

He'd have to apologize, the best way he knew how. There was no doubt in his mind that Randy would be mad. But maybe it wouldn't be too bad.

He just had to go, before it was too late. Before Randy realized he wasn't there.

Why didn't they understand that? Why couldn't they see that the longer he waited, the worse it would be? He glanced down at his lap. His hands twisted together without him seeming to make them move. He focused on them, worked at stretching his fingers out and then meshing his hands together again, as though he was a human puzzle.

Randy had a puzzle in his den. Shy had been curious. He'd picked it up and twisted it around, playing with the colors until he aligned them perfectly, one color to each side of the cube. But when he'd proudly showed Randy what he'd done, Randy had slapped the puzzle from his hands. And then he'd spanked Shy.

Shy exhaled a long breath and looked up again.

"Does Grant have any family that can take him?"

"Don't think so," Bobby replied.

"I'd like to go home now."

Until both men stared at him, Shy hadn't realized he'd spoken, that those were his words. Suddenly, he realized that's what he needed to do. "Please," he added, having almost forgotten his manners.

The men exchanged glances, although Shy didn't understand why there should be a problem. He needed to go home. He had to make the house ready. Randy wouldn't be long, and if he came home and things were not taken care of, there'd be hell to pay.

Bobby sighed and shook his head. He slammed his closed fist onto the top of his desk. Blankenship jumped, but Shy never reacted. "I don't see we have much choice. He can't very well stay here."

"I could take him home with me...." Blankenship began. Bobby vehemently shook his head.

"I wouldn't open that particular can of worms. Besides, I think being in familiar surroundings will do him more good."

"I still think he should be with someone," Blankenship insisted.

Bobby came around the desk and knelt before Shy. "Do you have any friends, Shy? Someone you can stay with?"

Friends? Shy shook his head. "I need to go home, please," he repeated politely.

"You know that Grant is a... monster." *Why does Blankenship sound so distressed?* Shy wondered. "How can we take him back there?"

"We have no choice. Shy's an adult. He's free to do as he wishes."

"Do you know what he was going to do? Do you have any idea?"

71

"I heard." Bobby groaned again and rubbed his face with both hands. "Oh damn, this is so hard."

Hard? Why was anything hard?

He had to go home. That was easy, not hard. If he didn't, *then* things would get hard. Then he'd get punished. He trembled at the thought.

Blankenship moved onto the couch beside Shy, laid his arm about his shoulder. "Shhh, shhh, it's all right, everything's all right, Shy. I'll take you home."

Home… home…. Yes, that's where he needed to be.

But just as he thought that, another idea entered his brain, and without stopping to think, he spoke the word aloud.

"Wyatt."

"WYATT, QUIT pacing. You're worse than an expectant father."

Wyatt stopped in midstride, turning toward his mentor. Lukas poured himself another shot and leaned against the back of the sofa, crossing his legs.

"He'll be here when he's here. You worrying about it isn't going to make it happen any sooner."

Wyatt's head was still spinning from the news they'd received. Or, rather, the call Lukas had gotten from Bobby Demaris. Telling them that asshole Grant had had a heart attack and been taken to the hospital and Shy was all alone and now someone was bringing him here.

Here. Why here? Because the only name Shylor had given them was Wyatt's. He gave Lukas a puzzled look. "How did they figure out to call you?" he asked again, as the first explanation had flown over his head in his excitement of hearing about Shy's imminent arrival.

"Boy, you need to calm down," Lukas chided him in a gentle tone. He patted the seat beside him. "Get over here before you wear a hole in the carpet and I'll tell you."

Wyatt didn't want to, but he did anyway, dropping onto the piece of furniture with little grace. That earned him another look, but

Lukas let the matter pass. "Shy must have told them you're living here, and since Bobby knows John, and knows he's out of the country, it only made sense to call me. Now, listen to me. Before he gets here, we need to discuss a few things."

"Discuss? Discuss what?"

"Well, how you intend to handle the situation, for starters."

Wyatt ran his fingers through his messy curls, trying not to tear out some of the strands in his frustration. He took a deep breath and attempted to focus on what Lukas was saying. This was too important not to. Shy's well-being depended on his keeping his cool.

"What do you mean?" he asked in a moderately calmer voice.

"I mean Shy's got to be traumatized, if for no other reason than he just watched his… saw Grant have a heart attack right in front of him."

Something flashed in Lukas's eyes, something resembling horror… or disgust…. Whatever it was, he didn't like it.

"What else? There's something else, isn't there? What happened to Shy at that club tonight?" He pronounced the word *club* as if it left an unpleasant taste, based on what he'd heard went on there alone. How could people live like that?

"Now, Wyatt, you have to promise me not to fly off the handle. And *do not* say anything to Shy about what I'm about to tell you. The only reason I *am* telling you is so you don't ask him about it. Got it?"

Wyatt nodded, not trusting himself to speak. He clenched his fists on top of his legs, bracing himself for the worst, whatever that might be.

"Here, drink this first." Lukas poured what little of the bourbon was left in the bottle into Wyatt's glass and held it to his lips. Wyatt tilted his head back and let the warmth trickle into his mouth and down his throat, sending reinforcement to his extremities.

"Apparently, from what Bobby told me, Randy and another guy got into it. Something to do with some business deal." He paused, looking down at his hands, then back up to Wyatt.

"And?" That couldn't be all it was. There had to be more to it, surely.

"And after they were threatened with being kicked out, they made up, and Randy…."

"And Randy what?" *Spit it out, already.*

Lukas took a deep breath and let the words out quickly, as if to deaden the impact. "Randy offered to have Shy blow a whole room full of men."

"*He what?*" Wyatt exploded. He leapt up from the sofa, his heart pounding, literally seeing red he was so angry. "That motherfucker! I'm going to kill him! Who the fuck does he think—?"

He found himself yanked unceremoniously off his feet and back onto the couch, before he could aim one of his fists toward the coffee table.

"What did I tell you?" Lukas didn't yell, didn't raise his voice, but his tone was too serious not to listen to, as if he was used to taking charge. Come to think of it, he probably was.

"Oh God, oh God, oh God," Wyatt moaned, then caught himself. Dammit to hell, Lukas was right. He couldn't fall apart now. Shy needed him. He was depending on him. And what was he doing? Losing his shit like a fool. Hadn't Shy asked for him by name? Didn't that mean something? Something very significant? What good would it do for Wyatt to fall apart on him?

He took deep, calming breaths, forced himself to focus. He had to know, to prepare himself for the truth. Whatever it was, he swore to himself, he wasn't going to react. He'd hold it in as long as it took.

"Did he… did he force Shy to…." He couldn't even get the words out. If he were to finish that sentence, he knew he'd be violently ill.

"No."

Thank God.

"Luckily, one of the other members intervened on Shy's behalf and questioned whether Shy was actually consenting or being forced."

"What did Shy say?"

Lukas shrugged. "Not much of anything. But that's when Randy had his heart attack, so it became a moot point."

Wyatt was glad on many levels, mostly for Shy's sake. "W-why... why would someone do that to another human being? Against his will?" Not that he'd be happy if Shy'd consented, but at least he'd accept that. But to be forced... that was just inhuman.

"Well, I honestly don't know. And, to be honest, I think, after tonight, Grant's worn out his welcome at the club, if that makes you feel any better."

"I'd feel a hell of a lot better if Shy got away from him. Permanently," Wyatt growled.

"Can't do anything about that right now, and that's nothing to worry about. Just keep something else in mind, Wyatt."

"What's that?"

"You can't touch him."

"What the fuck do you think I am, an animal?" Wyatt's indignation mounted, but at a glance from Lukas, he subsided into wounded silence.

"I didn't say that. Didn't even think it. But you honestly don't know what you're dealing with. It would take so little to scar that poor boy. And I'm not just talking sex here, though God knows that probably hasn't been pleasant. Just don't expect him to respond to you because you want him to. He won't appreciate it, and he won't know how to handle it. Take everything very slow with him. *Everything*, Wyatt."

"I just want to help him, Lukas," Wyatt said plaintively. "That's all. I have no ulterior motives. I'm not trying to get him into bed or anything. Honest."

"I believe you do care about him. Too much."

"What do you mean too much?"

"I think you're forgetting who he belongs to."

Another growl rose in Wyatt's throat. "That's ridiculous. He can't belong to anyone but himself. What kind of times do you think we live in?"

"You ask him that and you'll find out," Lukas said flatly. He laid a hand on Wyatt's arm, gazing earnestly into his eyes. "I know you mean well and you want to protect him. But what happens when he tells you he's going back to Randy? What happens when his Dom gets out of the hospital and claims Shy all over again? You have to realize that's going to happen. You can't afford to love this boy, Wyatt, you just can't."

"Maybe he won't get out." Wyatt clutched at straws. "People die from heart attacks all the time."

"Yeah and maybe that would be a kindness to Shy, but you can't count on that. And I don't believe you'd wish someone's death for that reason."

Wyatt set his mouth in a tight line and refused to let himself be drawn into an argument. Grant's death would not cause him to shed any tears, and he'd be no loss to the world. Most of all, Shy would be set free…. If that was a horrible thought, then so be it.

"So, what are you planning on doing?"

Good question. "Just keep him safe. Take care of him the best I can."

"With no expectations?"

"With no expectations."

"Good." Lukas let out a long breath. "That's a start. It's time for you to get your head together, if you really intend to do this, Wyatt. Shy needs a friend right now—he doesn't need a lover."

Wyatt saw the lights first, cutting through the darkness that blanketed the street. He jumped to his feet, almost falling in the process. A swift but gentle kick from Lukas reminded him to settle down.

"Why don't you answer the door while I clear up this mess?" He gathered up the empty bottles in one hand, picked up the glasses in his other, and quirked a brow at Wyatt.

"Yes, I know. Friend, not lover."

Lukas nodded, satisfied, and left the room.

It felt like an eternity but was probably mere moments later that the sound of the doorbell shattered the silence. Wyatt took a deep breath. *You can do this. You* have *to do this. For Shy's sake.*

Then he opened the door.

THE THOUGHT uppermost in Shy's mind was home. Getting home before Randy, making sure everything was immaculate. And preparing for his punishment. That he'd be punished, he had no doubt. Randy had told him to do something, and he'd not done it. There would be consequences—that Shy knew.

The man who drove him home was nice. He hadn't talked much, for which Shy was grateful. He'd asked Shy what music he liked to listen to. Shy said he didn't know much about music, so the man—who said his name was Bill—picked out a station. Shy didn't care what it was, he wasn't really listening.

When they walked up the path, only then did he realize that this was not home. But before he could voice his concern, the door opened and there stood Wyatt, and whatever Shy had been about to say evaporated, leaving him tongue-tied.

"Come in, come in," Wyatt welcomed them, standing aside. Bill motioned Shy ahead of him. Shy was unsure of what to do, but his feet had no such problem, and he found himself inside the house without having consciously decided to move.

Another man entered the room, from the direction of the back of the house. Shy recognized him. His name was Lukas. He was a friend of the man who lived across the street from them. He was also a member of the club. He was one of the Doms, like Randy.

Lukas glanced at Wyatt, then at Bill. Everyone seemed frozen in place, as though they were living statues. Wyatt broke the silence first.

"Sit down, Shy, please." He took a step toward him, then stopped, gesturing toward the sofa.

Shy reluctantly took a seat, to be polite, but he didn't sit back, hovering instead on the edge of the cushions. He didn't intend to stay for any length of time, so there was no need to get comfortable. Besides which, he was still a little sore from where Randy'd bitten him earlier.

"I have to get home," he repeated. Maybe if he said it often enough, it would happen. An image rose into his mind—two red-jeweled shoes clicking together, a voice intoning, *There's no place like home, there's no place like home*.... Shy instinctively pressed his own heels together tightly. Nothing changed.

Another awkward moment. When Bill cleared his throat, Shy thought Wyatt would jump out of his skin. The thought almost made him giggle, but he held it in.

"Sorry," Lukas apologized. "Wyatt, this is Bill Blankenship. Bill, this is my protégé, Wyatt Findley. You've heard me talk about him, I'm sure."

"Oh yes, definitely." Bill held out his hand to Wyatt, and Shy watched them shake.

"Thank you for bringing Shy. And for everything you did for him. I can't thank you enough...."

"You don't have to thank me. That was just—" He stopped speaking, glanced at Shy. "That was wrong on too many levels," he finished.

"Does he know—? I mean, has there been any word?" That was Lukas now.

Does who know what? Sometimes they seemed to be speaking just outside of his knowledge, as if they were discussing him and didn't want him to know what they were talking about. But why?

"I haven't heard anything, but frankly, I'm not interested in his condition," Bill replied.

Whose condition?

Before he had a chance to ask, the moment passed. Bill turned to him, an oddly serious expression in his eyes. Why was everyone acting so strangely?

"I'm going to be getting along. You're in good hands now, I can see that. You take care, Shy. And if you ever need.... No, I think you won't, will you?" He shook his head, as if to clear it. But his words made no sense to Shy. "I hope we meet again some time. Just not there." He stepped toward Shy and briefly patted his shoulder before moving on to the other two men in the room. He handed them a small card before shaking their hands. "Feel free to call me. Anytime."

"Thanks again," Wyatt said. "For everything."

Once Bill had gone, Wyatt returned and knelt before Shy. "Are you hungry? Would you like something to drink? Are you tired? Maybe you'd like to go to sleep?"

Sleep? Shy didn't think he was tired yet. But he had things to do.

"I should go home now." He patted his pants leg as a sudden thought struck him, producing a frown. These weren't his pants. No, how could they be? He'd not been wearing any when they'd gone to the club. Only a coat. And a cock ring. Where was his coat? He didn't care about the cock ring. Didn't care if he ever saw it again.

No, not true. If he lost it, then there'd be hell to pay.

"Shitfuck."

"What's the matter, Shy?"

Wyatt's voice was warm, like melted butter. Almost a verbal caress. Shy pushed the thought away.

"I don't have my keys. How'm I going to get in the house? I have to get in. I have to. I just have to…." The panic was overtaking him now. Just the thought of what Randy would do…. He released a small whimper, rising unsteadily to his feet. "I have to go," he kept repeating, as if by saying it the magic number of times, his wish would come true.

IT TOOK superhuman effort on Wyatt's part not to grab Shy and pull him into a hug. He wanted to comfort him so badly he could taste it, but Lukas's words still echoed in his ears. He bit his bottom lip until he couldn't stand the pain and kept his hands to himself.

It was hard, though, no shit. He could feel Shy's panic overtake him, and he knew what the problem was. He wanted to get back before Randy got there, afraid he'd be beaten for being absent or whatever other bullshit reason Grant might think of to punish him with. Shy hadn't comprehended yet that Randy was not coming home. Not tonight, anyway.

What could he do to relieve Shy's anxiety?

Shy's big blue eyes were pulling at his heart. He turned to Lukas. His mentor's expression was one of warning.

"I could probably get him inside…." He pitched his voice deliberately low, for Lukas's ears alone. He was thinking ahead, his half-formed thoughts tumbling over one another. He could break out a window. There were plenty of those, and he could repair any damage before Grant ever returned and he wouldn't have to know. He didn't like the idea of Shy being there, especially all alone, but if it gave Shy peace of mind....

Lukas shook his head. "I know what you're thinking, and that won't work. Don't you think that house has a security alarm? A damn expensive one? You'll just set it off, and not do yourself any good in the process...."

"Surely Shy knows the code—"

"Honey, I don't think he knows much of anything right now, to be honest."

Lukas was undoubtedly right. Shy seemed to be living in another world entirely. He had no idea what was happening around him.

Well, that worked out better anyway, as Wyatt hadn't really wanted to take him there, not to mention the idea of leaving him alone in that horrible place was beyond abhorrent. And he had no doubt it was a horrible place, just from the little he'd heard, and the little he'd seen of Shy and his.... Wyatt's mind refused to fill in the blank.

Okay, Wyatt, time to show a little maturity and actually deal with the situation at hand.

"Shy...." He touched his shoulder, softly, but didn't allow his hand to linger there, waiting a moment for an adverse reaction. There was none. One hurdle crossed. Best not to push his luck, though. "Why don't you stay here tonight? Tomorrow we'll see about getting you into the house, how does that sound?"

Shy gave him a blank look.

Wyatt held in his sigh of frustration. How could he reach him? More importantly, how could he do it without hurting him?

What was he doing wrong? Maybe the problem was Shy wasn't used to making any decisions on his own. Undoubtedly Grant did that for him. And with what Shy had been through, he was doubly unequipped to handle choices.

Well, then, Wyatt would have to do that for him. At least for now.

He rose to his feet, careful not to brush against Shy in any way. He didn't want to spook him.

"Come with me into the kitchen. We'll find something good," he said, keeping his voice firm but as gentle as he knew how. To his surprise, Shy made no argument and stood up from the couch. So far, so good.

He darted a glance at Lukas. His mentor gave him a nod of approval, saying nothing. Wyatt understood. The ball was most definitely in his court now.

Wyatt headed toward the hallway that led to the kitchen. He forced himself not to look back, trusting that Shy would follow him. Now he knew how Orpheus felt when making the long trip back from Hades, with the love of his life, Eurydice, trailing behind. And why he couldn't resist turning to make sure she was really there. And because he did, he lost her.

Wyatt didn't intend to lose Shy. Even if his common sense argued that Shy was not his to lose. He wanted him to be, though. Oh, how he wanted him to be.

The journey from the living room to the kitchen had never seemed so long. He opened the door to the pantry, and only then did he dare to look.

Shy stood there, patiently waiting.

CHAPTER SEVEN

WYATT ALMOST lost his train of thought, adrift in the infinite blue of Shylor's eyes. So large and expressive, even now, when his world must be crumbling around him. Why had he brought Shy to the kitchen? Oh yeah, to find him something good. Something comforting.

Something that wasn't him, no matter how much he wished it could be.

It occurred to him belatedly that loading Shy up with sugar might not be the best idea, not as late as it was. Wyatt had gotten the impression it wasn't exactly allowed in his diet, anyway. Maybe Randy was some sort of a health freak, *freak* being the operative word. But there was no sense in upsetting him unnecessarily when he had bigger problems to face. So maybe a big cup of hot chocolate, although warm and delicious, wasn't what was needed.

He opened one of the cabinets, searching for inspiration, and regretfully passed over the cocoa and marshmallows. His eyes lit, instead, on several boxes of tea bags, in assorted flavors. That actually sounded good. He'd make a cup for himself, as well as Shy, and a third for Lukas. Wyatt knew it wouldn't hurt to counteract all the alcohol he'd been throwing down with the hot tea. In his own defense, he'd had no way of knowing what was happening to Shy, even as he formed the basis of his conversation with Lukas. Had Wyatt known, he'd have been a lot more circumspect.

He selected a box marked Sleepytime and set it on the counter. God knows, they could both use the rest, although he didn't kid himself that it would be easy. With Shy around, Wyatt knew he was too keyed up to readily sleep, but if he was going to be of any use to Shy, he needed to make the attempt. Tomorrow would be a trying day as it was. Best to face it wide awake and in full control of what faculties he possessed.

He opened one of the lower cabinets and rummaged around before pulling out a medium-sized aluminum saucepan. That should be plenty big, he decided, looking between the pot and Shy.

"Fill this from the sink, will you?" He held the cookware toward Shy. "Then put it on a burner and turn it on high?" He tried to balance his tone somewhere between commanding and requesting, hoping to find a happy medium. One that would fall within Shy's comfort zone.

"Sure." Shy took the pot and proceeded to fill it from the tap, then placed it on the stove. Wyatt noticed that Shy clutched at the waistband of his pants as he reached for the dial that controlled the burner. They threatened to fall from his slender frame. No way those pants belonged to Shy. Wyatt was fairly sure he didn't want to know the story of how he'd come by them, either. But one thing was certain. Wyatt wasn't going to make him sleep in those oversized things. He'd find him something better to wear before bedtime. Luckily he had extra sleep pants. He could just lend a pair of those to Shy.

"Do you want me to get the cups?"

Shy's voice drew Wyatt from his reverie. "Thanks, but they're right here." He indicated the cabinet door with a wave of one hand. He'd barely gotten the words out when Shy reached past him and brought out three matching cups, in a delicate green floral pattern. He set them on the counter, placed an individual tea bag in each one, then found the utensil drawer and selected three teaspoons.

Boy, he's sure efficient.

His task completed, Shy glanced into the pot before he turned his face to Wyatt. His forehead was creased, and his big blue eyes seemed troubled. It took Wyatt a moment to figure out why—he'd done something on his own initiative, and he wasn't sure if he was to be punished for it.

"Thanks, Shy." He hoped his voice was as reassuring as it was meant to be. "I appreciate your help with the tea. You're probably better at it than I am, anyway."

Shy's face relaxed, and he pivoted toward the stove once more, his attention riveted on the water. Did Wyatt imagine it, or had a fleeting smile crossed that pretty face? His heart beat faster for just a moment at the possibility. He needed to focus on something else.

"Are you hungry? I could fix something…." He wasn't sure what there was in the fridge, but surely there was something he could quickly throw together. Or, barring that, he could always call out for some kind of delivery. Even if Shy'd had dinner, that must have been a while ago. As for himself, Wyatt couldn't remember if he'd eaten or not, and it didn't matter. He was more concerned with seeing to Shy's needs than considering his own. All he cared about was taking care of Shy, for as long as he was able.

"No, thank you" came Shy's quiet, polite reply.

Well, that answered that question.

When the water boiled, Shy distributed it among the three cups without waiting to be told. He picked up the box of tea and turned it about in his hands, glancing over the back. "Steeping time is three to five minutes," he informed Wyatt, probably assuming Wyatt didn't know. Which was an accurate assumption to make. "Want to set a timer?"

Wyatt had no idea if the stove even had a timer, much less how to use it, but he did know how to use the one on the microwave, so he set it for four minutes. "How do you take yours?" he asked Shy. "I have some sugar, or there's some kind of sweetener…." Somehow he knew the latter suggestion wasn't going to fly, and it didn't.

Shy shook his head. "Have any honey?"

That he did have. Masterson seemed fond of the stuff. In fact, he was well stocked with it. Wyatt nodded and pointed to a tall, open cabinet that housed an assortment of spices—some of which he'd never heard of in his life, bottles marked *marjoram* and *saffron* and *tarragon* and *cardamom*—as well as a miscellany of other foods. Such as honey. Shy found a small jar and set it near the waiting cups.

"This kind is good." Shy tapped the jar with one finger. "Natural. Very good."

If Shy was happy with it, then Wyatt was happy.

They stood together in a companionable silence while the tea steeped. Shy seemed lost in thought, his eyes affixed to the floor in quiet contemplation, and Wyatt didn't disturb him. Instead, he took advantage of his reverie to soak him in, fixing every angle and plane of his face, every point of his body in his mind for later. He wanted to sketch Shy, perhaps even do a painting. He'd much rather have Shy pose for him, of course, but he wasn't sure if he'd get the opportunity, or if Shy would even agree to sit for him, so he was committing as much of him as he could to memory. Just in case.

Between them, they carried the warm cups into the living room where Lukas waited and set them on the coffee table. Shy sat between Wyatt and Lukas, still poised at the edge of the cushions, as if ready to take flight at any moment. Lukas gave Wyatt a scrutinizing glance as he took his tea between his palms, letting it rest there, as if warming his hands.

Wyatt gave him a careful nod, as if to say so far so good. Shy remained silent.

"I called the hospital while you were in the kitchen," Lukas began at last.

"They talked to you? I'm surprised," Wyatt interrupted, earning him a look from Lukas.

"I told them I was his brother," he said tersely. "Anyways, looks like he's doing pretty well, all things considered, and he should be out of ICU and into a regular room some time tomorrow." He looked at Shy, then at Wyatt. Instinctively, Wyatt laid a comforting hand on Shy's leg, half expecting to be brushed off. Shy never reacted to the touch.

"Hospital?" Shy parroted Lukas. "What's going on?"

"Shy, I don't want you to be alarmed, but Randy had a heart attack tonight. While you were at the club."

"A heart attack?" Shy's voice was filled with confusion.

"Yes, but don't worry. He's going to be all right." Lukas focused his attention on Shy, who seemed unable to grasp the significance of what he was hearing.

"Does that mean—? He's coming home, right? I can't stay, I've got to—" He leapt up suddenly, knocking Wyatt's hand from its perch. Lukas gave Wyatt a pointed look. He quickly rose and reached for Shy, but thought better of it at the last moment and resorted to a verbal command instead.

"Stop!"

Shy jerked to a halt, frozen in place.

"Sit down, please. Drink your tea." Wyatt gentled his voice, even as an image flew through his mind—an iron hand in a velvet glove. He'd always wondered what that meant before, but now he thought he knew. He suspected it was a technique Lukas was more than passing familiar with, but it was all new to Wyatt. This whole scene. That's what this felt like. A scene from some movie. Except he'd lost his script and had no idea what his lines were, so he was having to ad-lib everything. Play it all by ear.

It was important to him that he get it right. For Shy's sake.

Shy trembled. For a moment, Wyatt wasn't sure he'd gotten through to him, but then he resumed his former seat, and a wave of relief washed through Wyatt when he picked up the tea and sipped at it. He hoped the warmth would be soothing. Belatedly, he wondered if he should have laced it with a little alcohol, to ease sleep. Too late to worry about that now.

"I'm afraid he won't be allowed any visitors tonight," Lukas interjected. "I should imagine they've given him something to keep him asleep. And it's too late for anyone to get into ICU now, anyway. Tell you what, Shy, I'll call first thing in the morning and talk to him. I'll tell him you're fine and we'll be there as soon as we know it's okay to be there. I'll make sure to tell him you're coming as soon as possible."

Wyatt realized it must be fear of retribution that fueled Shy's concern. Surely it wasn't because of any affection for that miserable wretch Grant.

Shy turned his troubled gaze to Wyatt, and Wyatt's heart melted at the sight, unable to resist the mute plea in those beautiful eyes.

"I'll be with you," he answered the unspoken question.

Shy seemed pacified at his response, his liquid eyes saying more than mere words could say, so it was worth it, he thought, even as he turned his head to face Lukas's inevitable glare and argument.

He tilted his chin defiantly and steeled himself for whatever Lukas might have to say. They locked eyes for a long minute before Lukas gave a reluctant nod, rising from the couch at the same time, placing his unfinished tea on the table.

"I'm going home, it's late. Tomorrow's going to be a busy day. You two get some rest. I'll see you tomorrow. I promise you, Shy, I'll… we'll get you to the hospital. Everything's going to be all right. Wyatt, walk me to the door." Not a request, but a command.

Wyatt knew what that meant—and it had nothing to do with Lukas needing directions. Lukas knew the house better than Wyatt did. He patted Shy's leg quickly. "Be right back," he promised before following Lukas to the door.

"What in the world are you thinking?" Lukas kept his voice low. One hand on the doorknob, his piercing gaze went straight through Wyatt.

"He needs me," Wyatt said simply. "I… I just want to be there for him, that's all. I'll stay in the hall, I promise. I won't let Grant see me."

Lukas shook his head, growling his discontent. "Just be careful," he said at last. "You may think you have a handle on this, but you really don't. This is deeper than you have any idea of. Trust me. And I don't mean the surface stuff. The leash, the collar, the flogger, the whip… those are just the tip of the iceberg, the outer trappings. It's a mentality. It's a way of life—" He stopped speaking abruptly and sighed. "Don't think about it tonight, okay? Just take care of Shy. And yourself. Get some rest. I have a feeling tomorrow's gonna be a hella long day." He pulled Wyatt into a quick hug, then let himself out.

Wyatt stood staring at the closed door, gathering himself both mentally and physically. Doubts crept into his mind, doubts fostered by Lukas's words. He was afraid… afraid of the damage he could do to Shy, whether intentional or not. Fear that he didn't know what he was doing. He was no psychology major—he was an artist, for God's sake. He painted what he saw on the surface, recreated images on canvas so others could see his visions.

But even as he crossed the room, returning to Shy's side, he realized he was selling himself short. Art was more than that. Each artist saw his subject differently, looked beyond the outward appearance, in order to bring out so much more, adding a little piece of himself in the process.

"You ready for bed?" He wasn't surprised when Shy shook his head. He didn't look sleepy. He clutched his teacup, held it close to his lips, as if drawing comfort from the warmth.

"Okay." Wyatt wasn't about to argue. "Want to watch TV?" That sparked no interest, either. Wyatt rubbed his fingers together, imitating Lukas's own habit, thinking, until an idea struck him.

When Wyatt had first moved in, he'd discovered that Masterson had a pretty sweet sound system, with speakers built into the walls throughout the house. Wyatt liked to channel music into the master bedroom at night. It helped him to sleep. Perhaps that could provide a soothing backdrop for them now. Approaching the tuner, he powered it on. The station was already set to a soothing jazz station. He adjusted the volume, wanting to keep it in the background. Maybe he could entice Shy into conversation. Or perhaps the music would lull Shy into sleepiness. At the very least, it might afford him a touch of serenity.

When he turned back to Shy, he found him standing, to his surprise, in front of one of the built-in bookcases recessed into the wall, scanning the spines. Shy touched one volume gently, almost reverently. He pulled it from the shelf, glanced at the cover, then opened it, his fingers caressing the pages with care.

Now Wyatt was curious. What book had put that look into Shy's eyes? He took a step toward him. Shy looked up, almost apprehensively.

"I'm sorry. I should have asked...."

"No, no, you don't have to, it's fine," Wyatt hastened to assure him. "Read anything you like." He took another step in Shy's direction, wondering if he'd move back, but Shy never stirred. That was encouraging. "What's that you've got?"

Shy closed the volume and held it up for Wyatt's inspection. Wyatt couldn't help but smile at the sight of the cover. *Alice's Adventures in Wonderland* was a favorite of his. "I love that book," Wyatt commented, producing an echoing smile from Shy.

"Me too," Shy confided. He opened his mouth, then closed it quickly, as if he'd thought better of whatever he'd been about to say.

"What?" Wyatt asked. "What were you going to say?"

"N-nothing." Shy bit his lip, then blurted out, "I just wondered if you would mind reading it aloud. It's just that you have this really great voice...." A blush rose in his cheeks.

Wyatt was more than flattered, he was shocked. Shy thought he had a great voice? Really? He was even more surprised he'd found the nerve to say so. How could he resist such an invitation? Of course he couldn't.

"Sure. I can use the practice." He wasn't even sure what that meant, but he added a wink for good measure, and Shy seemed satisfied. He padded back to the couch, still clutching the oversized pants by the waist.

"Hey, I have an idea. Maybe we should get ready for bed, in case we get tired reading? Those pants look... uncomfortable." He was trying to be diplomatic, and he didn't want to remind Shy of the circumstances under which he'd acquired them.

Shy considered the suggestion for a moment, cocking his head to one side, before he nodded. "Sure. That makes sense." He laid the book on the table and cast Wyatt an expectant look.

Emboldened, Wyatt crooked a finger at Shy, gave him an encouraging smile. "Follow me." Shy trailed him without question, up the stairs and down the hall where the bedrooms lay. "You can sleep here." Wyatt indicated the guest bedroom, which was next to the room he occupied. The single bed was made, and the room was neat and orderly, as opposed to the chaos that Wyatt had made of the master bedroom. He always excused himself by saying that a creative mind was a messy one. If so, then his creativity level must be off the charts.

"I have extra sleep pants." Wyatt rummaged about in the dresser Masterson let him use. Luckily he had two clean pairs left. He'd have to do laundry the next day, though. Assuming he could find the time. What with running to the hospital and who knew what after that.

One pair was a sort of burnished gold with a satiny sheen, while the other pair was red plaid. "Which color do you prefer?" he asked, turning toward Shy, one in each hand. What he saw took his breath away.

Shy had given up all attempts at holding the pants up and simply let them fall and stepped from them. Apparently he'd removed the T-shirt as well. All that remained was pure Shy… and Wyatt thought he'd never seen a more beautiful sight.

Shy had a slender build, but he was certainly not feminine in any way. Wyatt could see the definition of his muscles in his arms and chest, which tapered to a slender waist and flat hips. A pale gold treasure trail began just below his navel, and led south to where his soft cock lay partially hidden in a nest of blond curls. His legs were covered in a fine dusting of pale hair that matched his chest. There was something about his calf muscles that Wyatt found exceedingly sexy.

Shy pointed to the plaid pair, and Wyatt handed them to him, trying not to drool on himself or the pants. Shy seemed not in the least self-conscious, although he did turn his back to Wyatt before sliding his legs inside. Wyatt had to hold back his sharp intake of breath at the sight. Not the beauty of all that gorgeous naked Shy… but horror at the marks that marred that otherwise perfect back.

Dear God… what had Grant done to him? It looked as though Shy had been… had been…. He could barely force the word *whipped* into his mind, but that's surely what it looked like. Grant had beaten him or whipped him…. Wyatt thrust his fist into his mouth to choke back his words of protest. Good thing for Grant he was in the hospital, or Wyatt would have gladly put him there all over again.

A part of Wyatt's mind protested that this must be consensual. That Shy must like to be treated this way on some level. But another, saner part said no. How could he consent to something like this? How long had this been going on? How old was Shy… and that's where the crux of the matter lay. Had Shy even been old enough to give informed consent? Had he realized what he was getting himself into? Wyatt had an overwhelming desire to know the truth, but he knew that was something that couldn't be dealt with right now. Not tonight. He wasn't even sure when might be the right time.

His eyes flickered up and down Shy's body again, and he saw something he'd missed before. Marks on his ass. Not from a whip. If he wasn't mistaken, those looked like the impression of someone's teeth. Grant had… bitten Shy? That sick fuck!

Someday he'd make sure that asshole paid for what he'd done. No matter how long it took. But he couldn't think about it now. If he dwelled on it any longer, his brain would short-circuit.

By the time Shy turned back toward him, Wyatt had managed to regain control of himself and was now dressed in the satin sleep pants. Shy looked pointedly around the room, at the laundry tossed haphazardly about. Before he quite figured out how it happened, Wyatt found himself helping Shy to gather it up, and they pushed everything inside the hamper it was meant to go into. Wyatt didn't object. It was obvious to him Shy couldn't handle the messiness, so he let him have his way.

Afterward they returned downstairs without comment. Wyatt took one end of the couch, and Shy the other, each burrowed comfortably into the corner. Wyatt opened the book and began to read, attempting to breathe life into the ageless story of a little girl named Alice and her journey through a strange place known as Wonderland. Some things just never grew old.

Shy listened without comment. He'd taken one of the sofa pillows and hugged it to himself, an expression of contentment taking over his features. Wyatt glanced up at him now and then as he read, making sure he was still listening and that all seemed to be well. About half an hour into his reading, he saw Shy had fallen asleep. He stopped reading, waiting to see if the cessation of sound would wake him. Shy's head had fallen back against the couch, his lips were slightly parted, and Wyatt could hear his measured breathing. His face was even more beautiful in repose, reflecting none of the stress of his life. Wyatt's heart ached for him.

He laid the book aside and carefully started to pick Shy up, intending to carry him to bed. But suddenly Shy roused himself, gazing at Wyatt through sleepy-lidded eyes. So instead, Wyatt helped him to his feet and up the stairs to the spare bedroom. He turned down the blanket and top sheet. Shy crawled inside and rolled onto his side, as if he'd never been awake after all.

Wyatt smiled at the sight. "Good night, honey," he murmured softly, knowing Shy was beyond hearing. He left the door ajar, not sure how Shy felt about that, and kept a light burning in the bathroom, in case Shy woke and needed to use it. He felt silly for not having thought to show him where it was, but he couldn't do anything about that now. As he climbed into his own bed in the master suite, he wished he had the nerve to ask Shy to sleep with him. But he knew that wasn't going to happen any time soon. If ever.

It was sometime during the night that Wyatt became aware of another presence in the room. Startled, he snapped his eyes open, prepared for anything… except for the sight that met his wary gaze. There, on the other side of the bed, lay Shy. So close to the edge that with little effort, he'd roll off and hit the floor.

What did this even mean?

Wyatt wanted to reach out and touch him, but some vestige of common sense held him back, so he contented himself with soaking in the sight of Shy in his bed, and drifted back to sleep, thoughts of Shy dancing in his brain.

SHY HAD awakened into the darkness of a strange room. For a few moments, he couldn't remember where he was. This wasn't home, and it certainly wasn't the bed he shared with Randy. Although shared was a misnomer. Randy's bed was huge. An expensive king size, with intricate wood carving on the headboard and footboard.

When he and Doreen had first moved in with Randy, Shy had his own room, his own bed. But everything changed when Shy turned fifteen. When his body changed. His voice deepened. And Randy had begun to look at him in a different way.

Randy had always had charge of Shy's life, from the moment he moved in. This was just another facet of that. Doreen left and Shy moved into Randy's room. Randy wanted him there, wanted to keep an eye on him, as he called it. Shy did just as he was told and no more. Which included not masturbating whenever the feeling took him, but only with Randy's permission.

But Randy also liked having his space. He told Shy he didn't want to be touched when he slept. At first it was hard for Shy not to touch him once he fell asleep and rolled over. But after being beaten by Randy for touching him without permission, Shy had trained himself not to touch, to remain on the periphery of the bed, as far from Randy as possible. Together and yet not together.

Now he remembered where he was. Wyatt's house. And Wyatt was right next door, in the bedroom he'd helped him clean up.

Shy slipped from the bed. The floor felt chilly to his bare feet as he padded from the room, instinctively heading for Wyatt. He didn't know why, and he was too sleepy to analyze his reasons. He just knew that's where he needed to be.

He quietly slipped beneath the blanket, keeping himself on the edge, as usual. He didn't want to make Wyatt mad at him. He watched him sleep for a few minutes. Wyatt hadn't stirred once, not even when Shy's weight hit the mattress.

With a sigh of contentment, Shy rolled over and closed his eyes and fell asleep.

CHAPTER EIGHT

THE FIRST tendrils of morning light crept into Wyatt's awareness as he drifted to consciousness. He reached sleepily across the bed. Visions of Shy floated through his head, memories of him lying there beside him. So close and yet so far.

How badly Wyatt wanted to touch him. Wanted to pull Shy into the warmth of his aching embrace, to wrap himself about him like a living security blanket and keep him safe from harm. But his fingers closed only on emptiness, a coolness where he'd hoped Shy would be.

He cracked open one eye to confirm what he already knew—the other half of the bed was unoccupied. A feeling of panic welled inside of him, overriding the voice in his head, the one that managed to sound just like Lukas. He hadn't forgotten his mentor's admonition. He remembered Lukas's words very well—he just didn't know how long he could abide by them.

He threw back the covers and leapt to the floor, not bothering with his usual morning routine. Normally he took advantage of Masterson's king-size bed to stretch himself every which way but loose, to luxuriate in the feel of the soft, expensive sheets against his skin. Today he had other things on his mind.

Well, just one thing. Shy and his whereabouts.

Don't panic. He has to be here. Somewhere. Where else could he logically be? But Wyatt's heart refused to be reasoned with. It thumped erratically as he fled the bedroom and sprinted through the hall and down the stairs, skipping at least half in his haste.

The living room was spotlessly empty, the remnants of last night's drunken discussion with Lukas nowhere in evidence. The glass-topped coffee table gleamed in pristine innocence. Shaking his head in disbelief, Wyatt hurried into the kitchen. The unmistakable aroma of coffee hit his nostrils as he skidded across the floor, that and more. Something that oozed cinnamon and fresh-baked goodness. *What the hell?*

And there he stood. He was hunched over the counter, his nose buried in a book, his weight canted to one side so that Wyatt's sleep pants appeared in imminent danger of sliding down his legs at any moment. Not that Wyatt would complain if they did.

Shy glanced up. He blinked at Wyatt, pushing back a lock of blond hair that fell across his face, drawn from his literary reverie by Wyatt's dramatic entrance. Wyatt noticed what looked like flour on Shy's forehead. He had to resist the urge to dampen his thumb and wipe it away.

"Is something wrong?"

"Um, no." Wyatt attempted a casual air but knew he failed at it. Miserably. He was breathing hard and no doubt his face was red, and his normally messy hair probably looked even more unruly than usual, possessing that fresh-out-of-bed look that simply begged for a comb. "Um, what's that I smell?" *When in doubt, change the subject.*

"Cinnamon rolls. I hope you don't mind?" A fleeting shadow crossed Shy's face. His eyes were pinned upon Wyatt, his brow furrowed in unease, and for just a moment Wyatt found himself unable to speak, caught in that deer-in-the-headlights gaze.

Wyatt quickly pulled his head out of his ass. "That sounds wonderful," he reassured Shy. "Smells great. A lot better than anything I could do." He laughed in a self-deprecating manner. He glanced around the kitchen, a twinge of guilt hitting him at the realization that everything gleamed, there were no dirty dishes in the sink, and nothing out of place. Not even close to the condition he'd left it in.

I'd have gotten to it. Eventually.

Who was he kidding? He was a hard-core slob, and he knew it.

"You didn't have to clean."

Shy shrugged. "It's what I do." His eyes met Wyatt's in an unflinching gaze. Wyatt hated how he measured his self-worth by such ridiculous standards. But this was no time to lecture him.

95

"Well, thanks, much appreciated." He forced himself to break their locked stare and pulled out a mug from the cabinet. He poured himself a cup of coffee and sipped at the hot brew, hoping it would infuse him with wisdom along with much-needed caffeine.

Before he could draw upon his vast store of morning wisdom, Shy spoke up, hesitantly. "Is that your artwork in that room back there?" He indicated the rear of the house with a wave of one thumb.

"Um, what? Oh yeah. My art. Yeah, that's mine. I paint. Back there." Wyatt winced. Could he sound any more stupid? But Shy didn't seem to notice. He closed his book just as a quick beep, beep, beep resounded through the kitchen. Startled, Wyatt slopped hot coffee over himself before he realized it was just the timer on the microwave.

Shy straightened up and slid his hand into an oversized plaid mitt. He pulled a baking sheet laden with rolls from the oven and set it on top of the kitchen table, removed the mitt and laid it alongside, then went to the refrigerator and brought out a small bowl.

"I think you're really good, Wyatt." Taking a knife from the drawer, he began to swipe white frosting across the tops of the rolls. The confection melted on contact, and Wyatt's mouth watered. "I hope you don't mind that I was looking at your work." Shy glanced up, knife poised in midair. "I wasn't prying or anything, honest. I just thought I'd straighten up in there."

"Of course I don't mind. I'm happy you like it. It's what I do. It's what I go to school for." *Quit babbling already….*

A wistful expression laid claim to Shy's face, one of pure longing, but as quickly as it had appeared it was gone, and he couldn't swear it had been there to begin with.

Of course Wyatt didn't mind. He couldn't have been more thrilled at the idea that Shy admired his work. It fed his artist's ego and soothed his soul to find that Shy was interested in something he did. Perhaps, by extension, it meant he possessed an interest in the artist as well. At least Wyatt could hope that was the case.

Shy opened the dishwasher and brought out two small plates. He placed two rolls on one dish, a single one on the other, and set them on the kitchen table before going back into the refrigerator and emerging this time with a pitcher of orange juice. He poured two small glasses and set those by the rolls before giving Wyatt an expectant look.

Hastily collecting himself, Wyatt carried his coffee to the table and took a seat. "Wow, I didn't realize there was any juice in there."

"There wasn't. I made it."

Wyatt stared at Shy, openmouthed. Shy pinked a little and slid into his own seat without comment.

"Aren't you having coffee?" Wyatt broke off a piece of the roll and dipped it into his cup before taking it to his mouth. It was sinfully delicious and melted on his tongue.

"I already did. I can only have so much a day." Shy shrugged, as if it was no big deal, even as Wyatt was filled with the overwhelming desire to punch Randy Grant, over and over. That had to be *his* asinine rule. No normal person would live like that. He suspected no one had ever accused Grant of being quite normal.

He pushed away all thoughts of that unpleasant bastard. Randy Grant was the last person Wyatt wanted to have on his mind. Bad enough he'd have to deal with the subject later. But for right now, he wanted it to be just him and Shy—having breakfast, becoming comfortable with one another. And just maybe he could pretend this was their own little world, and enjoy their time together accordingly.

He quickly changed the subject. "These are delicious, Shy." Reaching for his juice, he took an appreciative swig. He'd never realized fresh-squeezed fruit could taste so much better than what he poured from the carton, but this certainly did.

He hadn't expected to have much of an appetite. Usually, the morning after, he tended to avoid food for the most part. But before he realized it, he'd eaten both of the warm and gooey rolls and was licking his fingers. His actions produced a small smile from Shy, who'd already finished his own breakfast. Wyatt had to refrain from urging him to eat more. He didn't want to make him uncomfortable. That would be counterproductive.

Shy started to rise, reaching for Wyatt's plate, but Wyatt stopped him, placing his hand over Shy's. "I'll get those. It's only fair. You cooked, I'll clean."

But he didn't move right away, and neither did Shy. They simply looked at one another, expectantly. Wyatt felt the warmth of Shy's surprisingly soft skin, despite the roughness to which it must be subjected. Shy's hand was delicate and yet strong. He wanted to cradle it in his own, to cover it with kisses. Wyatt knew he should move away before he did something incredibly stupid, something that would spook Shy. But damned if he could work up the psychic energy to do so.

He continued to stare into those fathomless blue depths and wonder what lay beneath them. He wanted to dive into Shy's soul and pull them both inside, escape into a world where no outsider could intrude. A place where there was no pain, no disharmony, no stupid rules, and no cruelty, only peace and love.

He wanted to capture Shy on canvas, explore what he felt for him through the medium of his paints. He wanted to express his passion for Shy without using the words he was forbidden to say—yet.

Shy seemed at ease with his touch, and Wyatt dared to hope that perhaps, in some small way, he'd gotten through to him. "Shy," he began, his voice so soft and hesitant he could barely recognize it for his own, "do you think maybe... I mean, would you be willing to—"

But the opportunity was lost when Wyatt's phone rang and he was forced to release Shy's hand in order to look for it, shattering what might have been.

Grumbling under his breath, he located the cell on the counter where he must have laid it last night, glanced at the caller ID before answering.

"Morning, Lukas."

"Good, you're up. You are up, aren't you? Not talking in your sleep?"

Wyatt pulled his lips into a wry smile that was lost over the phone, but his efforts were rewarded by an answering smile from

Shy. Maybe all was not lost after all. "No, we're up," he assured his mentor. "Didn't expect to hear from you so early, though."

"I hadn't expected to call you so early, trust me. Not after last night. But I got a call from a certain person this morning who is, shall we say, less than happy with life at the moment and is anxious to see his... that is, he wants to see Shy. As soon as possible."

Wyatt did an abrupt about-face at Lukas's words, hoping to hide the scowl that had immediately claimed his face. "Oh he does, does he? Well, isn't that just too bad!" His words came out more sharply than he intended. Damn that Grant and his lousy timing.

"Wyatt, don't be a brat. You knew he would. Or you should have expected it would happen, anyway."

"Maybe," Wyatt grudgingly admitted. "But I didn't expect it to happen quite so soon."

"I know, neither did I, but it can't be helped."

Taking a deep breath, Wyatt swung about again, forcing himself to give Shy a reassuring smile. Shy seemed uneasy, understandably so, considering Wyatt's erratic behavior. *Calm down*, he reminded himself.

"Okay, then," he resumed in what he considered a more reasonable tone. "How did he even know to call you? And where does he think...?"

"He called Bobby first and Bobby had the presence of mind to have him call me, thank God. As for Shy, Randy thinks he's with me and I didn't correct his assumption. But he is *not* happy, I can tell you that, and I guess I can't blame him. Last thing he remembers is having a major pain in his chest and then he wakes up this morning in the hospital, and he has no idea where Shy is or what happened to him."

Wyatt snorted inelegantly. "Don't even try to make me think he's really concerned."

"Whatever he might be, he's demanding to see Shy. I promised I'd bring him to the hospital as soon as I could, and I promised him it would be some time before noon. Gave him a song and dance about having to do something first, but I can't stall him forever. I'll come by about eleven and pick Shy up—"

"We'll be ready," Wyatt interrupted.

"Wyatt, goddammit, I don't think that's such a good—"

As they spoke, Wyatt had been closely watching Shy. He seemed to have gone pale, his smile no longer in evidence. Wyatt could feel him withdraw, closing up like a delicate flower caught in a chilling breeze.

"I have to go. Talk to you later." He clicked off without waiting for a response and reached for Shy. "What's the matter?"

THIS MORNING had been like a pleasant dream, warm and comfortable. In dreams, anything could happen, without repercussions. Shy was free to do as he wished, feel any way he wanted. He found that what he wanted was to please Wyatt—wanted to please him very much.

Shy had slipped quietly out of Wyatt's bed as he slept, so as not to wake him, not bothering to dress. He never wanted to wear those bigass pants again, not in this lifetime or any other. Wearing Wyatt's clothes—now that was something else entirely, even if they did feel a little loose. He didn't care.

In this dream, he could like Wyatt as much as he wanted and enjoy his company all he pleased, and no one could tell him otherwise. He could do things for Wyatt because he wanted to, not because he was being forced to. Making the cinnamon rolls was a break with the regimen he was forced to adhere to, something daring and hot and sweet… and didn't Wyatt appreciate them, as Shy had hoped he would? He had indeed.

And Wyatt was so talented. Shy wished he possessed a talent, wished he could do something special. But there was nothing special about him, and he knew it. In fact, it was his very imperfection that kept him where he was, for he couldn't do anything about it, and he couldn't change it. What was was, and that was just his life.

Shy pretended to himself they were playing house, him and Wyatt. Sitting in their elegant home, having a leisurely breakfast together. After that, who knew what they might do, where they might go. There were so many places in St. Louis alone Shy had never been.

They could visit those places, see what there was to see. At least in his imagination they could.

Shy was sorry the phone had interrupted Wyatt. Shy had a feeling he'd been about to ask something important. Maybe after he finished talking, he would complete his question. But he couldn't help but listen to Wyatt's end of the conversation, and reality washed over him like a bucket of cold water. And with reality, the truth struck him forcefully, tearing away the flimsy facade he'd constructed in his mind. What a fool he'd been.

The truth was he belonged to Randy—he'd been bought and paid for, thanks to Doreen. Randy was probably incensed that Shy wasn't at the hospital, waiting on him, seeing to his needs. Shy'd never been inside a hospital in his life and wasn't quite sure how things worked. But Randy wanted him there—that much was obvious from what he overheard. And the longer he delayed in going, the more hell there'd be to pay.

And what would happen when Randy got Shy home didn't even bear thinking about....

Shy assumed the mask once more. He sat in silence, his mind going blank. *Stop thinking about what can never be.*

Wyatt sounded concerned. Apparently his phone call was done. "What's the matter, Shy?"

"Nothing." Shy kept his voice deliberately cool. "Is... is Randy angry with me?" He flinched involuntarily at the thought.

"No, no, everything's okay. Lukas explained things to him. Everything's fine, Shy, please don't worry about a thing."

Wyatt clearly had no idea what Randy was really like, or he'd know how absurd that statement was.

"Lukas is going to pick *us* up about eleven."

Shy was careful not to show his relief at Wyatt's words. He knew he shouldn't want Wyatt to be there with him, but God help him, he did. He wasn't ready to let go of him quite yet. Whether he was willing to admit to it or not. As long as Randy didn't see Wyatt, then all would be well. Right?

He pushed the thought aside. Time to move.

Rising, he cleared the table, despite Wyatt's protestations that he wanted to help. Shy rinsed everything and set it inside the dishwasher. *Keep busy*, he told himself, *don't get comfortable*. When Wyatt attempted to engage him in conversation, he kept his responses short and atonal.

When there was nothing left to clean, Shy returned to the bedroom, the one he'd originally gone to sleep in, Wyatt trailing him. "I should get dressed, if we're going to leave soon." He eyed the sweatpants with distaste.

"I think I have something you can wear. Hang on just a minute." Wyatt ducked out of the room and clattering came from the next room. It sounded like Wyatt was turning the room upside down. Moments later, he returned and tossed a pair of jeans and a short-sleeved shirt onto the bed. "These should fit." He glanced down. Following his gaze, Shy saw he was looking at his feet, which were bare.

"I'm not sure my shoes will fit you," he admitted. "Let me see what I can find." And he disappeared again.

Shy took up the jeans and held them against his body. The length wasn't too bad. He could always roll up the cuffs. They were stonewashed, according to the tag, and they felt nice. He pulled them on and fastened them, then drew on the shirt, which was a light gray. He looked up as Wyatt reappeared, a pair of shoes in his hand.

"Here, try these on," he said. Shy sat on the edge of the bed. Wyatt handed him a pair of black leather shoes with black laces and a pair of black silk socks. Shy slipped on the socks. Then he pushed his foot inside the left shoe. It was slightly big, but not too bad. Just a little wriggle room.

"Mr. Masterson has smaller feet than I do," Wyatt explained, almost apologetically.

Shy drew on the other shoe, tightly laced them both, and stood. "Does this look okay?" he asked, craning to peer behind him. It didn't really help. He couldn't see a damn thing. He stopped twisting and glanced back at Wyatt. Wyatt had fallen silent. He stared at Shy as if he were trying to memorize him or something. Shy found himself caught up in his hypnotic gaze.

Holding his breath, he swayed toward Wyatt, unable to fight the pull of his attraction.

"Shy…." Wyatt whispered. He took a step toward Shy.

Shy knew that any moment now their bodies would collide, and he braced himself for that collision, dreading it and wanting it both. *Just one kiss.* First and last kiss. He'd never kissed anyone but Randy, and those touches had become cold long ago. Why did he think Wyatt's touch would be warm in comparison?

Just before they came together, a loud chime sounded. Wyatt swore and Shy pulled back, trembling.

"Damn! Hold your water, Lukas," he muttered under his breath, reaching out for Shy.

But the spell was broken. Wide-eyed, Shy backed away from him, his lips moving, but no words forming. Frustrated, he gave up and ran for the stairs and the safety of the front door.

That had been too close for comfort.

CHAPTER NINE

THE HOSPITAL complex was enormous, a myriad of gleaming white buildings that sprawled in every direction. Shy knew if he should become separated from Wyatt and Lukas, he'd be lost. He couldn't begin to imagine finding his way back to this place on his own, and he trembled inwardly at the idea Randy might demand it of him.

There were so many people here, employees and visitors alike, the only difference between them lying in the way they were dressed. Too many people for Shy's comfort level. He didn't do very well in crowds. Normally he never had to deal with them. The most people he usually came in contact with were the ones at Shop for Less, and he wasn't even very comfortable with them. This was just agony.

He huddled close to Wyatt in the elevator as they rode it up to the sixth floor. They stood together in the rear corner of the car, Lukas having taken a position just in front of them, as if shielding them from the other passengers. Shy was grateful for the older man's presence. Lukas had always been nice to him at the club, never leered at him like so many of the others. Never treated him like a piece of meat. And he never accepted the sexual favors Randy was so liberal about granting at Shy's expense. He tried not to think about how many men had touched him, how many he'd had to suck off, whether he was willing or not. Consent was never in question, as it was not his choice to give it. If he did think about those men, he didn't think he could live with himself.

Wyatt's hand covered his own. Warm and comforting, it imparted much-needed strength. When had he taken possession of Shy's hand? It didn't matter, it felt good. And right now Shy needed that, so he could face what was sure to come. Randy was bound to be angry, and he would have questions regarding Shy's movements. He'd want to know *every*thing, and Shy didn't want to *tell* him everything, but he wasn't sure how not to. And if Randy found out about Wyatt… correction, *when* he found out about Wyatt… there'd be hell to pay.

Still, as much as he dreaded the coming conversation, he also wished it done and over with. He needed to take what was coming to him, and he needed to get back in the house, back to his lot in life. He didn't deserve to be any more than what he was—Randy's possession. His unpaid indentured servant for life. How foolish of him to pretend, even for one moment, he could be anything else.

Shy glanced up in surprise when Wyatt squeezed his hand. "Don't worry about anything." Wyatt pitched his voice for Shy's ears alone. "I'll be right outside, in the hall, if you need me. Just give me a sign and I'll be there."

I can't do that….

Shy didn't bother to state what he considered to be the obvious, drawing illogical comfort from the idea Wyatt would be close at hand. Common sense said he should make him wait somewhere else, keep him as far away from Randy as possible, but his heart wanted Wyatt near, and he found it hard to fight the feeling. So he simply nodded, the conflicting emotions inside of him making him queasy. He hoped he wouldn't throw up, not here and definitely not there. Randy would regard that as a sign of weakness. He'd yelled at Shy as a child whenever he was sick and couldn't make it to the bathroom. And he'd always made him clean up his own mess. Told him it built character.

They exited the elevator into a maze of corridors crowded with people. Nurses pushed carts laden with covered trays and uniformed maintenance people swept the floor with push brooms, agilely dodging patients and visitors alike. Shy couldn't keep track of the path they took, even by following the numbers and arrows stenciled in black on the walls. He had the illogical desire to drop breadcrumbs behind them to mark their path, just so they could find their way out again.

They stopped suddenly near a large round area marked Nurses' Station. Obviously not Randy's room, so why were they here? He glanced at Wyatt uncertainly, but Wyatt seemed as clueless as Shy.

"Wait here just a minute," Lukas said. "I want to make sure he's ready. I promised I would." He gave Wyatt a look that Shy couldn't fathom before continuing down the hall. Wyatt shrugged.

"I'm sure it's no big deal," Wyatt tried to reassure him, but Shy's stomach told him otherwise. "Maybe he wants to make sure we're not interrupting anything. Like the doctor. Or a nap."

Randy considered naps a sign of weakness, but Shy saw no reason to mention the fact. He clenched his free hand to anchor himself. The other was still tightly tucked inside of Wyatt's for safekeeping. He focused his attention on the floor, staring at the diamond patterns in the black and white tile as if trying to memorize them. He jumped at a sudden clatter and looked up. A blonde nurse with bright red cheeks stood near them. A metallic clipboard lay on the counter where she'd slammed it down. Shy could almost see steam rise from her in angry waves.

"Let me guess." A second nurse, a short-haired brunette seated on the other side of the desk, greeted the first one. "His Highness not find lunch to his satisfaction?"

"Told me he didn't eat pig swill and I could just throw it to the pigs!" the blonde seethed. "Wanted me to call his personal dietician so she could bring him *real* food. Do you believe it? And then he had the balls to tell me that if I insist on holding him prisoner here, the least I can do is to feed him properly! What nerve!"

The brunette made a noise that could be loosely interpreted as sympathetic, but Shy thought it sounded more like choked laughter. The feeling in the pit of his stomach intensified. Could it be…?

"Bethany, I don't suppose you would—" The blonde's voice turned plaintive.

"Save your breath." The brunette held up one hand, as if to stem her colleague's words. "I feel your pain, but no way do I want to switch with you for him. He's done nothing but bitch from the moment he woke up this morning. He may be hot, in that older guy kind of way that I normally like, but that man is all kinds of messed up."

"Don't I know it?" the blonde grumbled. "With my luck, I'll be stuck with him into next week too."

"Better you than me, honey. Cheer up. I'm sure they'll let him go soon. Not like he needs surgery or anything." The brunette openly laughed as Shy's stomach did a nosedive. Oh hell. He was sure they were talking about Randy.

And if that was true, then Randy was in a bad mood. A *very* bad mood.

He squeezed Wyatt's hand without thinking and then just as suddenly dropped it. What was he doing? He was begging to be hurt. If not now, then later. Worse, he was laying Wyatt open to becoming the object of Randy's rage. He couldn't let that happen.

"Shy, what—" But before Shy could verbalize any of his emotions—something he was not used to doing—Lukas returned. By the look on his face, Shy's worst fears were being realized.

"Um, yeah, let's go on in, why don't we?" There was a definite level of discomfort in Lukas's voice. Shy took a few deep breaths to calm himself as he prepared to face Randy, assuming his mask of practiced indifference.

"Let's go." He didn't dare to risk a look at Wyatt, afraid he'd undo all his hard work. At least he could do that much—spare Wyatt's feelings, even if he was good for nothing more.

As they moved away, he heard Lukas mutter, "Don't, you'll only make things worse." He couldn't help but wonder what Wyatt had wanted to do, but it didn't really matter, did it?

Shy didn't know what to expect when they entered Randy's room. Other than to be yelled at. That much was a given. The first thing he noticed was the cleanness of the room. Everything gleamed whitely, from the floor to the walls to the bedding on the two beds in the room. Shy said a mental thanks to the powers that be—one less thing for Randy to be unhappy about. Unfortunately, there was bound to be something else.

The bed on the far side of the room lay empty. A hooked white plastic curtain hanging on a track that ran along the ceiling was pulled back to expose the neatly made bed. Closer to them, to the left of the door, was the bed that must be Randy's, although he wasn't in it.

Instead, Randy sat in a chair beside the bed, his lips set in a thin line. Shy's heart dropped at the sight.

Shy forced himself not to react to Randy's appearance, although he should have been prepared for it. He'd had a heart attack, and that was serious business. Truth be told, though, Shy hadn't known what to expect. He'd never really seen Randy ill or looking less than his best. He'd always been careful about that—Shy wasn't sure why. Certainly not out of consideration for Shy. Now Randy seemed… pale? Or was that weak? Maybe it was the harsh lighting of this rather sterile room. That was it, surely. What else could it be?

Shy moved to the end of the bed automatically. He stood at attention, facing Randy. From this vantage point, without making any obvious effort, he could see into the hallway where he knew Wyatt waited. He even imagined he could see Wyatt's shadow, there against the far wall. The idea was a comforting one. The important thing was not to stare or be obvious in any way.

"I called you. More than once." Randy's voice dripped with accusation.

Shy had been staring down at his feet, waiting for it, expecting it—it being Randy's displeasure. And now he obviously had it. He glanced up to meet Randy's deepening scowl.

"My phone's in the house." Shy wasn't even sure why he bothered trying to explain. It never seemed to make a difference. Right or wrong, Shy was always sure to be wrong and Randy right.

This time was no exception to that long-established rule.

"Where *you* should be."

Shy swallowed but offered no explanation. He couldn't help staring at the machines that surrounded Randy's hospital bed, some of which appeared to be hooked up to him. He'd seen a few medical shows in his time, enough to know that wasn't a good thing. What exactly was wrong with Randy, and how bad was it?

"That's why we're here." That was Lukas. Shy appreciated his effort, valiant as it was, but he could have told him to save his breath, Randy would never listen. "To get the key to the house, remember? You have it, Shy doesn't."

Randy's face grew darker. Shy braced himself, surprised Randy hadn't moved out of the chair yet. Probably because of the restraining tubes that came out of his arms. Normally he'd have begun punishment by now. Maybe his inability to get up quickly was a good thing. At least in front of Lukas.

"So he's been with you, has he?" Randy narrowed his eyes, looking over Shy's head to where Lukas must be standing, just behind him. Perhaps Lukas wanted the same view of the hallway Shy had, although for different reasons. Shy cut his eyes toward the hall and quickly back.

Shy's heart beat faster, waiting for Lukas's response. He hadn't been, of course. Hadn't been with Lukas. He'd been with Wyatt. Yes, Lukas had been there, at least at first. But most of what Shy remembered was Wyatt, both last night and today. And that knowledge would not sit well with Randy, not at all.

"Of course I've been looking out for Shy," Lukas said smoothly, so smoothly that Shy himself almost believed it to be the unvarnished truth. He dared a quick glance at Randy to see what he thought. He didn't seem any angrier. Surely that was a good sign?

"How... how are you feeling?" Shy ventured to ask. It seemed the thing to say, under the circumstances, but the question felt odd on his tongue. He'd never had to ask it before. Apparently, though, he'd said the wrong thing, as Randy's brows drew together and he glowered again.

"Don't let this crap mislead you." He waved one arm, and the tube moved with his gesture. "There is nothing wrong with me," he insisted. "*Nothing.*" Despite Randy's protestations, Shy could read between the lines and discern what Randy wasn't saying—the message was right there in his glare. *Just you wait until I get you home.*

Words he'd heard from Randy more than once in his life.

Shy barely refrained from shivering. Showing weakness in front of Randy would not help in any way, only exacerbate the already awkward situation. He stole a quick glance toward Wyatt's shadow and back. Still there. Good. He drew comfort from the knowledge, steeling himself for more of Randy's anger and/or interrogation.

"Please don't get excited, Randy. It's not good for your—" Lukas began.

Randy started to rise from the chair. Shy hadn't paid attention to Randy's wardrobe before, but now he realized he wore only a loosely fitting thin print gown and nothing else. A far cry from Randy's usual expensive attire. And not very flattering.

Shy took a half step back, running up against Lukas, who encircled his waist for one brief moment, then hastily removed his hands as he stepped around him, placing himself between Shy and Randy.

"I mean the machines might come unbalanced if you move too much."

Shy wasn't sure what Lukas had originally meant to say, but he didn't think that was it. The question was, would Randy buy into that?

Randy resettled himself in the chair, and Shy prayed that the moment—whatever it was—had passed, holding his breath to find out, one way or another.

"Get out here where I can see you."

Shy quickly stepped forward as Lukas scooted aside, standing at attention once more. Randy raked up and down his body with a critical eye.

"Those aren't your clothes. Whose are they?"

Before Shy could summon the wits to think of a plausible answer that wasn't the truth, Lukas had interceded once more.

"He couldn't get in the house, remember? You've got the key, naturally." *Because you're the boss.* The undertones in Lukas's words were clear. "We had to make do with what we could find until he can get back home."

Randy narrowed his eyes and chewed on Lukas's words for a moment as Shy resisted the urge to rock back and forth on the balls of his feet. *Stand still, don't fidget,* he cautioned himself. When Randy nodded a grudging acceptance of the necessity for the change, Shy breathed a silent prayer of relief.

"Those go in the garbage as soon as you get in. And cleanse yourself thoroughly. I don't want any trace of them on you when I get home. Is the house in order?"

110

"Yes, Sir," Shy replied automatically, although his brain protested he hadn't been able to get inside to do anything. But common sense reminded him that neither had anyone else had access, and it had been immaculate when they'd left—was that really only last night? It felt a lot longer ago, for some reason.

"Is the food any good?" Lukas waved toward a cart on the far side of Randy's bed. Shy's heart sank. He already knew the answer to that question.

"No, it's swill, fit only for pigs." Randy snorted his contempt. "I tried to explain my dietary needs, but the bitch wasn't interested. Another reason for leaving here as soon as possible."

"Have they told you when you're getting out?" Lukas asked. The question produced another scowl, Shy wasn't sure why.

"Damn hospital. No one gives me a straight answer around here. The most my... doctor says is maybe in a few days. Maybe a week. But damned if I intend to stay here that long. The food's inedible, and this bed is like sleeping on rocks...."

"At least you're not sharing a room?" Shy applauded Lukas for attempting to put a good spin on the situation. He didn't think it would work, though, and it didn't.

"Thank God for small favors, right?" Randy's tone was anything but grateful. Shy thought he sounded more than a little aggravated, which was never good for anyone.

"The nurses are incompetent, at best," he continued in an aggrieved voice. "They seem to think they have free rein to treat me like I'm some sort of human pincushion. Either that or they're all working on a Girl Scout voodoo badge and using me to gain extra Brownie points." He glanced down at one arm, then the other. "They ignore me when I summon them and then dare to show up when I don't want them. They're surly and sarcastic and totally without manners. Oh, there'll be some letters written once I get out of here, you can count on that."

What had happened to the other Randy, the one who charmed everyone he met and never allowed anyone to see his hidden nature? He didn't seem to be in evidence at the moment. Perhaps it was this

111

place. Or maybe it was the heart attack? Shy had become disillusioned about that man long ago. Maybe Randy wasn't bothering to hide himself for Lukas's benefit because Lukas knew him too well too. And Randy obviously didn't give a damn what the hospital employees thought about him.

Typical Randy.

"I expect you to stay busy." He turned his attention back to Shy.

Of course. What else had Shy expected? Randy always insisted he stay busy. He had a saying about idle hands that he was fond of beating Shy over the head with at every opportunity. Bet it was coming now.

"Idle hands are the devil's tools, they say. And while I may not believe in a horned red bastard with a bifurcated tail, I do believe that idleness leads to trouble. And we want you to stay out of trouble, don't we?" His smile was so insincere and rather weak—a pale imitation of his usual megawatt grin. Still, it was enough to make Shy squirm.

He cast a surreptitious glance through the door and back. Good thing Randy didn't know—

"What in the hell is so damn interesting in that hallway?"

Shy froze, tongue-tied.

WYATT WANTED to pace so badly he could taste it, but he didn't want to move from the spot where he'd taken up residence, across the hall from Grant's hospital room. He'd promised Shy he'd be there for him, and he would be, no matter what. But not knowing what was happening, and not being able to hear a damn thing inside those four walls, was wearing on his nerves. The only thing that held him together in the slightest was the knowledge that Lukas was there, and that Lukas would watch out for Shy. Surely even Grant didn't dare to do anything that Lukas might bear witness to.

But then he remembered what he'd been told of the events at the club the night before, and he slowly began to lose his mind all over again.

He leaned against the wall, shifting his weight from one foot to the other, worrying about what was going on, wishing he could hear what was being said. Nothing but the murmur of voices drifted into the hall. None of whatever conversation they might be having was audible. Wyatt trusted Shy would call him if he needed him, but what if he couldn't?

Maybe if he edged closer to the door....

Before he could put his impulsive thought into action, perhaps exposing himself to Grant's view, Lukas exited the room, closing the door behind him. Wyatt sprang up, freed from his inactivity at last. Passionate words bubbled to his lips, but Lukas was already shaking his head.

"Don't start. I didn't have a choice. He said he wanted to talk to Shy alone. What could I do?"

Wyatt stared from the closed door to Lukas and back again, panic seizing him. He grasped Lukas's arm in an iron grip, until the other man shook him off.

"Get a hold of yourself. Quit acting like an idiot and calm down. It's not as bad as you think."

"Not as bad? Not as bad?" A passing nurse gave Wyatt a cold eye, and he lowered his voice as she walked on. "What happened in there? What did he say? What did he do?"

"Just asked some questions, wanted to know what Shy's been doing. Where he's been. What did you expect? He controls him, you know that. Naturally, he's trying to reassert that control." Wyatt noticed Lukas's glance dart away from him to some indeterminate point farther down the hall. Distraction? Or avoidance?

"What happened?" Wyatt repeated. "Something bad, wasn't it? Tell me, please, I need to know."

Lukas's answer was too halting for Wyatt's taste, as he listened impatiently. "It could... have been... better," he admitted. "But it also could have been a lot worse. For Christ's sake, Wyatt, I took him in there wearing your clothes, having spent the night with you. And"— he held up one hand—"I'm not asking, and I don't want to know what happened between you. That's none of my business. But...."

"But…?" He didn't want to hear, but he had to know.

"Randy caught Shy looking out in the hallway and asked him what he was looking at. Of course, I knew it was you, but neither one of us was about to admit to that. Luckily, I think I diffused the situation with a little quick thinking. That's when Randy said he wanted to speak to him alone, so I left." Lukas shrugged. "If you're worried he'll hurt him, don't be. They've got him pretty well wired up. I'd be more worried about when he gets home."

"When will that be?" Wyatt dreaded the answer.

"Well, considering it's Friday, probably not before Monday. They don't release people on the weekends. Not even obnoxious ones. Might be as long as a week."

"That seems awful fast." Wyatt had been hoping for a lot longer than that, to be honest. "Don't they have to do surgery or something?"

"No, he told me that when I called earlier. He's here more for observation than anything. They want to play it safe, considering he's so young, and considering he did have a heart attack."

"If he doesn't need surgery, then what? Why would someone his age have a heart attack?" The idea didn't make much sense to Wyatt. He'd assumed Grant had a bad heart. What other causes of heart attacks were there? He refrained from making any further comments on Grant's age. He'd learned his lesson on that one.

"I don't know, but I can make an educated guess, between what Shy's said and what Bobby's told me."

Wyatt tried not to roll his eyes. Was he going to make him ask the question? Apparently so. "What? What's your guess, Lukas?"

"Apparently he likes to pop Viagra."

"Viagra?" Wyatt hadn't seen that coming. "You mean… he can't get it up by himself?"

Lukas snorted. "No, that's not what I mean. There are some people who take it who don't really need it, they just like the effects. You know, that four-hour hard-on that won't quit. They find it impressive."

Wyatt couldn't imagine that, but then he'd never had trouble getting an erection in his life. And never wanted one that lasted four hours. "So…?" There must be more to it than that, although the idea that Grant had trouble getting a stiffy tickled some perverse sense of humor.

"So like any drug, if you abuse it, there can be consequences. I suspect he might have double dosed. And the heart attack was the result. Hush now."

Startled, Wyatt glanced toward the open door. He clamped his mouth shut when he saw Shy emerge. It took all of his self-control—along with Lukas's restraining hand—to keep from grabbing Shy and hugging the stuffing out of him.

There, the ordeal was over. Wyatt breathed a sigh of relief. Now he could take Shy home and minister to him, work on this fledgling relationship he felt growing between them. Nurture him and care for him, heal his broken bird….

But wait, something was wrong. Shy's face was a marble mask, and his eyes… dear God, what was that look? So cold… so cold….

Shy marched straight up to Lukas, his back so straight you'd have thought he had a ramrod for a spine. "I'm ready to go home now," he said in a voice that pierced Wyatt's soul like a sharp piece of cold steel.

Something had happened. Grant had said something or did something, pushed Shy over a precipice, threw him back down into the hole Wyatt had worked so hard to pull him up out of. He wanted to scream. He wanted to curse everyone and everything he could think of. He wanted to throw something and watch it shatter into a million pieces. But some vestige of maturity that existed somewhere deep inside held him back.

Lukas's eyes held pity, as well as understanding, and something else that Wyatt could clearly read: *I told you so.*

Goddammit, maybe he had, but that didn't mean Wyatt had to like it.

The two turned away. Shy never looked at Wyatt, never acknowledged his presence, never spoke a word. He followed them in silence. The elevator ride down seemed infinitely longer than the one up. Shy stood by Lukas, on the far side of Wyatt. If Wyatt moved toward him, he edged away. Finally Wyatt gave up in despair.

The ride back to the house was equally as silent. This time Shy rode in front, beside Lukas, while Wyatt languished in agony in the back seat. Lukas pulled in front of Grant's house and turned to the silent Shy.

"You have the key, right? Randy gave it to you, didn't he?"

Shy nodded.

"Is there anything you need, anything I can get you?"

Shy shook his head.

"Thank you for your help." The voice was so faint Wyatt could barely make out the words. "I'll return the clothes after I wash them." He addressed all his remarks to Lukas, still ignoring Wyatt.

"You can keep them," Wyatt said. Shy never responded. He reached for the door handle and murmured something so soft that Wyatt wasn't sure he'd understood him correctly. Not until he left the car and walked stiffly up the front walk, quickly disappearing through the front door, did his words register in Wyatt's brain, and he gave Lukas a look of pure horror.

I guess I'll see you at the club....

Dear God, what was going on? And how could he rescue Shy from this atrocity when he seemed determined to remain caught in the web?

CHAPTER TEN

SHY DROPPED back onto his haunches and swiped his shaky hand across his damp forehead. He panted, drawing air in ragged gasps. His skin reeked of bleach and ammonia. His knees ached, and he was sure the pattern of the bathroom floor tile was permanently etched into his flesh.

He'd begun to clean the moment he entered the house. Not that the house was dirty, but that had nothing to do with anything. Fear was his motivation. Fear and conditioning. Not wanting to piss Randy off, and not wanting to be on the receiving end of his reprisals for even the hint of an infraction against his rules. Shy didn't want to be tied up and locked in the Blue Room again… or worse.

Battling these fears was his need to forget—to stop feeling, stop caring, stop thinking… about anything. To push away the emotions and sensations he didn't understand and didn't know how to handle.

But every time he thought he'd brought himself under control, an image would appear in his mind's eye and impale itself upon his heart, and he'd come undone all over again.

Wyatt's gentle smile. The warmth and humor in his eyes. The kindness he'd displayed to a virtual stranger. The way he'd championed Shy, braving Randy's ire.

Remembering Wyatt and the time they'd spent together, Shy's heart ached, and tears cascaded down his cheeks. Then he pushed himself even harder, as if manual labor were a cure for what ailed him. As if he could scrub his agony away with the hard-bristled brush he used to scour the bathroom floor.

He was an idiot, that's what he was. A fool to ever think someone like Wyatt… that Shy could ever be good enough for someone like him… that life could ever be any different than what it was now.

But then he realized that it could and would change... and all for the worse... when Randy came back.

Changes, he'd said. There would be changes. But he hadn't elaborated, and Shy hadn't bothered to ask. Knowing what was coming wouldn't make any difference. It wasn't like he could change anything. Whatever it was, he would have to endure it. Somehow.

He scoured the toilet until the porcelain shone, scrubbed the bathtub until he could see his reflection in the immaculate surface. Not that he bothered to notice how he looked. The bleach fumes made his head spin, and his common sense told him to step outside and get a little fresh air, but he was afraid to do that. Afraid that if he opened the front door and took a step in that direction, he might not be able to stop.

He lifted the bucket full of dirty water and lugged it to the kitchen, struggling to keep the contents from sloshing out with every awkward step he took. He hoisted the pail up on the edge of the sink and balanced it there for just a moment before he started to tilt it inward. At that moment the house phone rang. Shy jumped at the unexpected sound. He knocked the plastic bucket into the sink. The handle clattered against the faucet as it spilled its contents. The water swooshed out in an angry gray deluge that surged momentarily, then swirled down the drain.

His first thought was Randy—checking up on him—and a shudder ran through him. But then he realized that didn't make sense—Randy would call his cell if he wanted to contact Shy, never the landline. So who could it be?

He grabbed a kitchen towel from the drawer and wiped his wet hands before reaching for the cordless phone on the counter. The caller ID display read *Tony*, and Shy breathed a sigh of relief. It was just Randy's trainer. Oh shit, it was Friday, wasn't it? Where'd the time gone? It was Randy's regular workout day. Obviously that wasn't going to happen.

"Grant residence." Shy's greeting was automatic, despite knowing who was on the other end of the line. Randy had trained him well. "How may I help you?"

"It's Tony," came the expected response. "I'm outside, but the door's locked. What's up? Where's Mr. Grant?" He sounded impatient, a tone Shy knew he'd never use on Randy. With him, he was deferential, and butter wouldn't melt in his mouth. He didn't waste manners on Shy.

"He isn't here." Shy knew better than to elaborate. Randy had made it clear no one was to know anything about where he was or what had happened to him. He hadn't explained why not, and Shy hadn't questioned him.

"What do you mean he isn't here? He's expecting me." Shy could hear the growing irritation in the trainer's voice, but it was nothing to do with him. And there was nothing he could do about it, or wanted to do.

"He said he'd call you when he wants you." As an afterthought, Shy asked, "Is there any message for him?" The line going dead was his only response. Shy wasn't surprised. The trainer was a veritable Neanderthal, and thinking wasn't his strong suit. Another reason not to confront him. He had a feeling the other man would be quick with his fists, and he wasn't about to put himself in a position where he could use them. Let Randy deal with him later.

As long as he was here, might as well clean, he thought.

He repeated his performance in the kitchen, even took a bucket of scalding hot water and thoroughly cleansed the inside of the dishwasher until it looked like it had just come from the factory, and then he tugged and yanked at the refrigerator so he could get behind it. Floor, walls, ceiling. Every cranny, nook, and corner he could easily reach and then the ones that were hard to get to. By the time he was done, he was sweating bullets, but he could say with certainty that everything was immaculate and could stand up to the rigors of any examination. Even Randy's.

Then he started on the other rooms. In between vacuuming and dusting and sweeping, he ran loads of laundry, made sure every item of clothing Randy owned was clean. He folded everything just the way he'd been instructed before he set it carefully back into Randy's drawers. Everything on his dresser in its rightful place—Randy would know the difference if it weren't, and he'd do something to Shy about it. Shy would give Randy no cause for complaint—not if he could help it—and he knew that he could.

Besides which, if he focused on the Herculean tasks he set for himself, perhaps he could keep the other thoughts at bay.

He wasn't sure what time it was when he heard the doorbell. He wasn't really sure he'd heard it at first, ascribing it to a combination of his imagination and wishful thinking. He was running the vacuum underneath the cushions in the living room at the time. But when the ringing was repeated, and then became insistent knocking, he couldn't ignore it, and his heart started to beat wildly, despite his best efforts to calm it.

Just a delivery, just a delivery, he assured himself. He started toward the front door but paused, irresolute. Then he darted to one of the front windows and peeked cautiously out. That's what he'd been afraid of. No brown van sat in front of the house, no driver in crisp uniform shorts to be seen.

Wyatt, go, go go.... He dropped the edge of the curtain and leaned against the wall, shaking. *Please, please, please.* He closed his eyes, hugged himself, and held his breath. He thought he heard Wyatt's voice calling his name, but he ignored it and eventually the sound died away.

Shy took a deep breath, told himself it was for the best, and went on with his chores.

WYATT ANTICIPATED he'd be on the receiving end of a lecture from his mentor after Shy bolted from the car. It had taken all his willpower not to leap out and race after Shy, to find out what was wrong, what had spooked him. Lukas forestalled such a move by quickly pulling away from Grant's house and parking in Masterson's drive, where he hurried Wyatt inside.

Wyatt braced himself for another round of admonitions of what he could and couldn't do, as in *don't touch Shy, be careful what you do and say, you don't understand what's going on, they live in a whole different world*, etc. But it didn't happen, much to Wyatt's chagrin. He'd expected to be berated. He wanted Lukas to tell him what to do so he, in turn, could let everything bunched up inside of him out. He wanted to scream and shout, to argue, to extemporize on the evils of Randy Grant. To hear Lukas agree that Grant was a bad man and he didn't deserve to have Shy in his life, that he was bad for him, and he didn't even know the first thing about how to treat another human being. Most of all Wyatt wanted to brainstorm with Lukas. Between them they should be able to devise a plan to get Shy out from under that sadist's thumb for good. They had to, for Shy's sake. It was the only humane thing to do. How could Wyatt even consider leaving Shy in a blatantly dangerous situation?

But that didn't happen. Lukas had stayed only long enough to down a quick cup of tea, then said he was leaving so Wyatt could get down to business. And by business he meant art. That subject Wyatt was majoring in and intended to make a career out of. The portfolio he was working on so Lukas could arrange showings for him, maybe even a one-man art exhibit. Some day. Hopefully in the not too distant future. He needed to think about the coming school year and what classes he was taking, where he intended to go from there. He was too close to graduation to screw up now. And clearly Shy didn't fit into that game plan, at least not in Lukas's opinion.

In other words, *get on with your life*. The way Lukas looked at him spoke volumes, more than his words. Wyatt read the message clearly contained in his eyes: *forget about Shy, he's beyond anything you can do to help him. Focus on your art. Some things just are.* It was not meant to be unkind nor unsympathetic, simply realistic.

But Wyatt was an artist, not a realist. His world was not quite so black and white, even if Lukas seemed to have forgotten what it was all about. Maybe he was too old for love. Or too cynical. Wyatt considered himself neither one.

After saying he'd be in touch soon, Lukas saw himself out. Wyatt never stirred. Lost in reverie, he leaned over the kitchen counter, head bowed, arms pressed against the smooth surface, his own cup of tea sitting forgotten in front of him. His mind was filled with thoughts of

Shy and what he must be going through. Could Lukas be right? Was he doing more harm than good by remaining in Shy's life? That was the last thing Wyatt wanted to do.

And yet his heart argued that it wasn't true. Shy had seemed more alive when they were alone together, more at ease. Wyatt was sure he'd gotten through to him, touched him in some way. Hadn't he come to Wyatt's bed of his own volition? That had to mean something, surely. Shy had seemed to be doing all right, more than all right in Wyatt's company. Up until the time when he'd been forced to make an appearance before his tyrannous lord and master.

And that was the problem in a nutshell. Grant was obviously no good for Shy. He was a controlling asshole who thought of a sweet young man as his possession, who didn't see him for the amazing person he was. He poisoned Shy's world simply by being in it. And the sooner Wyatt removed Shy from Grant's sphere of influence the better.

The question remained—how was Wyatt going to do that? More importantly, would Shy *allow* him to do it? When it came to Grant, Shy seemed unable to think beyond what he was told to do. Could he possibly have been brainwashed by the older man? Or was it simply that living the lifestyle Lukas had spoken of had affected his thinking and turned him into a numb automaton? There was so much Wyatt didn't understand about their situation, he realized. He wanted to learn more, including how Shy had ended up in Grant's clutches, but Lukas had effectively told him to leave Shy alone, so he couldn't expect any support from that quarter. He didn't know where else to turn.

He reached for his tea, but it had gone cold. Well, that was an easy fix. He straightened up and stretched his back. Then he placed the cup inside the microwave and set it to heat for thirty seconds. While it warmed, he stuck his head inside the refrigerator. It occurred to him he hadn't eaten since that morning, not since he'd risen to find Shy had made fresh cinnamon rolls. And not from a can, which was generally the only kind Wyatt ever got unless his roommate went to the bakery. Shy had placed the leftover rolls into a plastic container for later. Looking at them, thinking about the time they'd spent together, made Wyatt miss him all the more.

Had Shy eaten? Was he taking care of himself? What was he doing? What kinds of things did he do when Grant wasn't around to monitor him? Wyatt didn't know, and not knowing was haunting him.

It wasn't until he found himself on the other side of the street, standing at the front door, that he realized he'd acted entirely on impulse. He'd gone from wondering if Shy had eaten to deciding to invite him out for a late lunch in the blink of an eye, his feet carrying him where his mind had already gone. What could it hurt, right?

He pressed the bell and listened for the answering echo as it resounded inside, while he waited for Shy to answer the door. But he never came and the door never opened. So Wyatt resorted to knocking, and finally, in desperation, to calling Shy's name in a voice filled with concern. No movement from inside. Although, for a moment, Wyatt thought he saw one of the curtains move. Continued silence was his only response.

Finally he gave up. Shy wasn't speaking to him, whatever his reasons. No sense in standing there forever. If he'd been thinking more clearly, he'd have brought something to write a note, slide it beneath the door or something. But he hadn't. Maybe later.

Returning to the house, he headed to his temporary art room. He pulled out various works in progress—some still in the sketch phase and others having been worked in either watercolors or oils— and made halfhearted attempts to continue with them. He considered himself an artist of the old school, and he related most closely to the Impressionists, particularly Monet, albeit with his own modern take on the Impressionist style. He loved landscapes the best, particularly those that possessed a surreal, almost fantasy feel to them, although he was known to work with figures as well. But today nothing looked right and nothing felt right. And every single blue was a pale imitation of—and an insult to—the crystal clarity he saw in Shy's eyes. And they all faded into insignificance beside the original.

Even when he gave in to the desires that dominated his creative mind and tried to put the image of Shy that filled his inner eye onto paper, the results were feeble and poor in execution. He crumpled each one and tossed it to the floor, snorting at himself in derision.

Finally he gave that up too as a worthless cause and settled in front of Masterson's huge flat-screen television, holding the game controller he'd brought with him in his lap, as he lost himself in his favorite online role-playing game. Every time he shot or bludgeoned one of his onscreen foes, he imagined it was Randy Grant, and the thought brought him a certain measure of satisfaction.

But not nearly enough, not compared with the loss of Shy.

He thought about going to the store to get something for dinner, but decided to make do with what he already had on hand, afraid that if he left, Shy might need him for something and wouldn't be able to reach him. Futile hope that was, he knew.

He discovered a partial bottle of Moscato he'd forgotten about in the back of the fridge, and he drank it with the frozen pizza he heated up for dinner. Afterward, he turned the stereo system to a classical station and curled up on the sofa in the living room with Holst and a book a friend had sent to him as a must-read. Gay men, nasty aliens, and dinosaurs—something you didn't read about every day. For a while he lost himself in the fascinating world of Berit and Tom, but his mind kept returning to Shy.

At last he carried the book and the last of the wine to the bedroom, set them on the bedside table, undressed and went to bed, tossing and turning until at some point Morpheus claimed him and he fell asleep.

He had no idea how long he'd been lost to slumber when he felt the bed shift beneath him and realized he was no longer alone. Startled, he opened his eyes into the darkness of the room, his heart beating faster. Was he imagining things, or was it wishful thinking that caused him to see Shy where he wished he was? But when he realized it really was Shy, the knowledge floored him. He was almost afraid to breathe lest he disturb the delicately balanced figure on the far side of the bed, facing away from him.

Shy was here—he was really here.

Wyatt couldn't believe he was actually seeing him, but there he was, there lay Shy, silhouetted in the dim moonlight that filtered through the curtains. And then Wyatt realized what had awakened him as he came more fully to awareness. Shy's slender frame shook, as if he was crying.

"Shy...." Wyatt had to speak, had to say something, so Shy would know he wasn't alone, that Wyatt was there for him.

The shaking ceased, and Wyatt thought he heard a stifled sob. Then Shy slowly rolled over, and Wyatt saw a shudder rack him, and his heart ached for him. He reached out one arm toward him.

"I'm here," he whispered.

For a long, agonizing moment, he thought he'd scared him away, as Shy began to move again. But it was toward him, not away, and this time he didn't run from Wyatt. He curled up against him, his face pressed into Wyatt's chest, as he sobbed into Wyatt's strength. Wyatt absorbed the tremors without complaint, cushioning them even as he gently stroked Shy's back.

"Shhh," he whispered gently, "I'm here... I'm here...."

Wyatt held on to Shy as if he'd never let him go, waiting and listening for the sound of his even breathing, to know that he'd fallen asleep at last, before he finally closed his own eyes and joined him in slumber.

CHAPTER ELEVEN

SHY COULDN'T blame this time on confusion.

He'd purposely exhausted himself, scrubbing the house from top to bottom—including the Blue Room, which held its own special brand of terror, even without Randy's menacing presence. He tried to scour away the memory of Wyatt's voice as he'd pounded on the front door, pleading with Shy to answer it. He hadn't been trying to hurt Wyatt. He rationalized his actions as a necessary evil—necessary for both their sakes.

Too tired to think, he'd finally decided to call it a day. He stripped off his sweat-stained clothes, took a quick shower, and crawled into the single bed in the guest room. Once upon a time it had been his bedroom—before Randy made other sleeping arrangements for him—but no trace of his former self remained. Nothing that hinted that a child had once slept there. Although guest room was actually a misnomer, for there were never any guests in this house. Randy would never permit that.

Sometime in the middle of the night, Shy had awakened to the oppressive silence of the house. It threatened to engulf him, like a living tomb. He didn't want to be there—he knew what he wanted to do, where he wanted to be. Half-asleep and acting on sheer instinct, he pulled on a pair of pants and a T-shirt, forgoing shoes, and stumbled across the street.

To Wyatt.

He fortuitously found the front door unlocked. He pushed it open and quietly slipped up the stairs to Wyatt's room, stripped and slid beneath the blanket, lying on the edge of the bed.

He lay there for a few moments, hardly daring to breathe, afraid the raspy sound might wake Wyatt. Already he began to doubt the wisdom of what he'd done. Not the reason, but the ramifications. The knowledge of what would happen to both of them if Randy found out terrified him.

He felt more confused than he'd ever been in all his life. He was frightened, and he didn't know what to do.

Harsh sobs attempted to tear loose from his soul. He stifled them as well as he could, but his best was not good enough, as usual, and he felt the bed shudder in protest. And then he heard the voice of an angel—at least it sounded like one to him—and he was drawn into the most forgiving warmth he'd ever felt, and he surrendered to it, spilling his liquid fears until he'd no more to give and he fell into blessed sleep.

Warm breath that prickled the back of his neck was the first clue Shy had that he was not alone when he awoke. Momentarily confused as to where he was, he knew he certainly wasn't with Randy, for if he ever got this close to Randy he'd be quickly and harshly shoved to the other side of the bed. If not kicked to the floor.

Besides which, Randy was in the hospital.

No, this was not Randy's breath that warmed his skin in rhythmic pulses, for Randy's breath was icy and reeked of wintergreen, like the mints he kept in a case in his pocket. And this was not Randy's strong arm wrapped about Shy's torso like a protective mantle, for Randy's limbs were lean and hard, meant to inflict pain and not to dispense tender caresses. And this certainly was not Randy's bed. This bed already felt more welcoming to Shy in the two times he'd slept in it than Randy's had at any time over the past five years.

Wyatt.

Shy hardly dared to breathe, afraid if he moved the spell would be broken. Afraid to open his eyes and truly awaken only to discover it was all a dream and none of it was true. That he was really still under Randy's thumb, inside Randy's house—Randy's possession.

But then the memory of where he was filtered into his conscious mind, and a sense of wonder filled him at his own audacity. Or was that foolishness?

From behind him, Shy heard a soft moan and he tensed, anticipating a blow. But nothing happened and the moment passed. The bed shook beneath them. Shy felt Wyatt roll over, heard him mumble something, his words muffled by sleep.

Shy cautiously followed Wyatt's example and eased himself over, trying not to disturb Wyatt by the movement of the mattress. He didn't want to signal he was awake. Wyatt lay on his back, one arm bent, his hand pressed against his forehead, eyes closed. Still very much asleep. Shy breathed a silent thanks as he studied him without fear of observation or reprisal.

Wyatt's hair lay in loose curls that framed his face. Such a beautiful, rich shade of brown. The color of cinnamon, Shy decided. He'd always found something comforting about that particular spice. Perhaps that's why he'd chosen to make cinnamon rolls for Wyatt. Sometimes he sprinkled a little on his allotted coffee ration, inhaling the combined fragrances before he took a sip. But only when he was alone. Randy would have called it foolishness. And probably found an excuse to take it away. Not that he needed an excuse—Randy's word was law.

His own blond hair looked so lifeless in comparison to Wyatt's. So straight. Nothing special, it hung just below his shoulders. At Randy's insistence, he kept it tied back. His preference, not Shy's. It had been a lot longer at one time, almost reaching down to Shy's ass. Then one day Randy had cut it. A punishment for something he didn't like. Shy couldn't remember now what he'd done then. He just remembered sweeping up the little pieces of himself afterward, doing his best to hide the ache in his heart. He told himself it would grow out, but he also knew all Randy had to do was say the word and he'd be sheared again. Like a lamb to the slaughter. After that, he'd kept it shoulder-length.

Wyatt always seemed so at ease with himself and the world around him. Even the perpetually tousled look he wore, which might have just looked messy on someone else, suited him. Shy envied such confidence. He knew he didn't possess it and never could.

The morning sunlight glinted off some of the strands, making them appear almost red. Shy reached out a curious hand without thinking, caught himself, then hastily withdrew it. *Mustn't touch. Not allowed.*

He never touched Randy without permission. Not that he wanted to. Even at the beginning of their—relationship—his sexual curiosity had been tempered with fear.

He'd once looked on Randy as a father figure, probably for lack of any other male in his life who could be said to fulfill that role. He hadn't known any better. He was just five when his mother had moved them into Randy's house, and he honestly couldn't remember a time when they hadn't lived there.

Perhaps the idea that Randy was his father had been a natural assumption to make. For as long as he could remember, Randy had been the one to discipline him, as Doreen couldn't be bothered. Randy had been the one who taught him to read, the one who homeschooled him.

He'd also been the one who gave Shy the rules he expected him to live by.

Shy had learned the hard way, though, that Randy was indeed not his father. First when he'd called him that and Randy had reacted in what he came to know as typical Randy fashion. That was the first time Randy spanked him with his belt. One with a very large, very hard buckle.

The night Randy brought him into his bed only confirmed that fact, as Randy taught him what was expected of him. These were not fatherly terms of endearment by any means.

And the lessons just kept on coming.

"Penny for your thoughts."

Shy started. He glanced up fearfully. He'd been so lost in his own head and the unpleasant memories he couldn't repress he hadn't noticed Wyatt was awake. Now Wyatt regarded him with those intense blue eyes, the ones that Shy thought he could happily drown in.

In another life, of course. This one was spoken for.

Shy didn't know what to say. He sure wasn't about to tell Wyatt what he'd been thinking about. No need to go there. Luckily, Wyatt didn't seem to expect an answer. Maybe the question had been rhetorical.

"Looks like it's gonna be sunny today." Wyatt squinted toward the window. Shy wondered what time it was. He'd undoubtedly overslept, at least according to his usual schedule. But it didn't seem to matter today. Today felt different.

"'Course it's St. Louis, that could change." Wyatt chuckled. "I know I heard the weather guy give the forecast last night, but damned if I can remember what he said." He pushed the blanket aside, bunching it up between them, and stretched out his body to its full length with a satisfied grunt. "They're usually wrong, anyway, you know?"

Shy couldn't help but notice that Wyatt was very naked. And very hard. *Must be morning wood*, he reasoned. Certainly nothing to do with his presence in Wyatt's bed.

"Did you sleep okay?"

Shy nodded, forcing his eyes away from the riveting sight of Wyatt's erection. His stomach clenched in a knot of apprehension. If Wyatt asked why he'd come here, what would he say? How could he explain his impulsive action to Wyatt when he didn't actually understand it himself? He'd probably just sound stupid if he tried. Better to keep busy so he wouldn't have to answer any awkward questions.

"I'll go make breakfast," he volunteered and quickly rolled over. Away from the sight of the naked Wyatt. He started to drop his feet to the floor, but Wyatt's words arrested him.

"No, that's okay. There's still some rolls left in the fridge. We can heat those up. I'll make us some coffee. Unless you'd rather have something else?"

"Oh, okay. No, coffee's good. Well, then I'll clean the house while you—"

"You did that yesterday. House looks fine, Shy. Better than I've ever kept it."

Shy was momentarily flummoxed. If Wyatt didn't need him to cook breakfast, and he didn't need him to clean the house, what did he want him to do?

Of course, what everyone wanted from Shy. What he did best. It was the least he could do considering he'd broken into Wyatt's house in the middle of the night. A business transaction, nothing more.

He slid deftly across the bed in one serpentine motion, his hand snaking out to encompass Wyatt's hardness. It was warm to his touch, pulsing against his palm.

Shy pumped Wyatt's cock quickly a couple of times before changing positions, bending purposefully over his body, his hair veiling his face from view. He moved his hand and deftly ringed the base of Wyatt's erection with his fingers to make room for his mouth as he swallowed as much of Wyatt as he could get in one gulp. He had no fear of gagging—he was a master of deep-throating.

He began to bob up and down on Wyatt's shaft, sucking hard. Moans of pleasure emanated from Wyatt, and he squirmed beneath Shy's expert ministrations, proof he was doing a good job.

So focused was he on what he was doing that the hand that grabbed his hair took him by surprise.

"Stop!" Wyatt's hoarse voice cried.

To say that Wyatt was taken by surprise by Shy's actions would be an understatement.

To say he didn't enjoy what Shy was doing—the pleasurable sensations that coursed through his body as Shy sucked on his cock—would be an outright lie.

Oh God, what a talented mouth Shy had. Wyatt could feel already feel his toes starting to curl. It had been a long time since he'd been with anyone, much less anyone so good at what he did. At first he let his second brain do all the thinking. Intelligible speech was out of the question. The only sounds he seemed capable of producing were guttural moans.

But then his first brain actually managed to engage, and he realized just how wrong this really was. He couldn't let it go on, no matter how much he wanted to. It took all his self-control not to simply revel in the pleasure he was being offered. But it was for all the wrong reasons, and he knew it, and he could *not* take advantage of Shy in that way.

Wyatt was *not* Randy Grant, and he never wanted to be mistaken for that slimy bastard, in this lifetime or any other.

He had to stop this and he had to stop it now. Before he reached the point of no return and wasn't able to. He didn't want Shy to think his only value lay in sexual subservience. Far from it.

His hand reached toward Shy. He meant only to tap him on the shoulder, but at the last moment his aim was deflected and he ended up gripping his hair, another shudder of pleasure passing through his frame as he finally got out the reluctant command to stop.

In afterthought, Wyatt realized he was lucky not to have startled Shy into biting him. As it was, Shy pulled back immediately and raised his head, bright blue eyes wide in surprise. Wyatt winced at his confused expression. He felt as though he'd just kicked an innocent puppy.

Shy crawled backward, away from Wyatt, his stricken gaze never faltering. Acting quickly, Wyatt pressed his hand against Shy's cheek before he moved too far away.

"Oh God, babe, please… don't look at me like that. It's not that I don't want you. I do, I swear it—"

Words failed him, and the few he'd gotten out sounded weak, even to him. In the back of his head, he could imagine Lukas's voice, hear the accusations, delivered in scathing tones. *Didn't I tell you to butt out? That you'd only hurt him?*

Fuck this.

He could order Shy to stay where he was, he could tell him to move closer… to do just about any damn thing he wanted… and Wyatt knew it. He'd proven before that if he used the right tone it would work, as if Shy were conditioned to obey—which he probably was, come to think of it. But that was not how he wanted their relationship to begin. And he had no doubt in his mind that they *would* have a relationship. A real one. Not whatever sick, twisted idea of one Grant had brainwashed Shy into having for the past five years.

A real, loving relationship, based on mutual trust and respect, on basic human decency, something Grant knew nothing about, obviously.

Which only strengthened his resolve not to let Shy go back to Randy Grant—ever. Even if he didn't know just how he would accomplish that.

"Please," he said softly. "Please don't go. C'mon up here. So we can talk. Just talk."

Shy froze in place. Wyatt could only imagine how confused Shy must be, how conflicted.

"I won't stop you from going, if that's what you really want to do. But I wish you would just give me a chance...." *Give us a chance.* But he was afraid to speak those words aloud, afraid he'd only scare him even more than he already was. One step at a time. One step.

Waiting for him to decide which way to go was going to be a real test of Wyatt's patience. But he'd do whatever he had to do in order to win Shy's trust.

It felt like an eternity, but was probably only a few moments later that Shy inched up the bed, maintaining his distance from Wyatt, who was trying to gather his thoughts. Before he could say anything, Shy broke the momentary silence between them.

"Did I do something wrong?" Wyatt thought he detected a note of panic in Shy's voice, as if he was afraid of being punished. He could only imagine why he felt that way.

"No, of course not," Wyatt hastily assured him.

"Then why...?"

"Because you don't *owe* me that."

"But I do," Shy protested. "I broke into your home in the middle of the night. Into your bed. I have an obligation—"

"*No!*" Wyatt's voice came out sharper than he'd intended and he quickly softened his next words. "No, Shy, no. You never owe me anything for that. I'm here for you. Remember, I told you that? I'm your friend, not...." He flailed for words before blurting out, "I'm not that fucking asshole."

Shy made no immediate response. Wyatt felt him tremble, and his heart ached for him. He remembered what Lukas had told him, that Shy had been living with Grant since he was just a child. This had to be hard for him, as difficult as it was for Wyatt to grasp the kind of life Shy must have been leading. Even though Lukas had tried to explain the lifestyle, he just didn't get why someone would allow themselves to be put into that kind of situation to begin with, much less stick with it.

Perhaps because he didn't have a choice?

Maybe that was the whole problem in a nutshell. His mother had left him there, for whatever reason, with that lunatic control freak, and Shy didn't know anyone else, had nowhere else to turn. Well, dammit, he knew someone now, and Wyatt vowed he'd keep Shy safe with him, no matter what.

"Hey," he said, reaching out despite his best intentions not to touch Shy and stroking his cheek. "I have an idea. You want to jump in the shower real quick while I make breakfast? Well, heat it up." He laughed, hoping to relax Shy's tension. It seemed to work, at least somewhat. He stopped trembling. "You can borrow some of my clothes again." He answered the unspoken question in Shy's eyes.

"And then what?" At least Shy seemed interested enough to ask. That had to be a step in the right direction, surely.

"And then we'll just have fun."

Shy looked pointedly at Wyatt's obvious erection. "Don't you want me to—"

Wyatt was afraid he might not be strong enough to resist a second attempt. Yes, he wanted to touch Shy, wanted to be touched by him. But not yet, it was too fast. He wanted there to be more between them than sex, even if it was right there, waiting to be had.

He pulled Shy to him and pressed their lips together, his only intent being to still the offer before it was actually made. Occupy Shy's mouth in some other way. But his purpose backfired as a warm current flowed between them, and he found himself reacting to the kiss more deeply than he'd expected, fueled by the taste and scent of Shy. When Shy unexpectedly breached Wyatt's mouth with his tongue, Wyatt felt a moan travel between them, one he recognized as his own. And now it was Wyatt who trembled at Shy's touch, Shy who seemed to be calling the shots.

Only the fortuitous ringing of Wyatt's cell kept the situation from progressing to the next stage. Shy pulled back, his expression unreadable. "I think I'll take that shower now."

"Good idea," Wyatt concurred. He was gratified to see that he was not the only one with a hard-on as Shy padded out of the bedroom and headed down the hall, Wyatt's eyes fastened on his swaying ass. "Fresh towels are hanging up!" Wyatt called after him. He took a deep breath, rolled over, and reached for his phone, grabbing it just before it went to voicemail. Lukas, of course. Who else?

"Did I catch you at a bad time?" his mentor drawled. "You weren't sleeping, were you?"

"No, no, not asleep. Why, what's up?"

"Just checking on you, that's all. Seeing if you're okay. Are you okay, Wyatt?"

"I'm fine, just fine, Lukas." He heard the sound of the water turning on and tried not to think of Shy's naked body beneath the warm spray. He had a feeling if he chose to join Shy in the shower, he wouldn't be turned away.

To forestall such a move, he put the phone on speaker and set it on top of the dresser while he grabbed a pair of sweatpants and yanked them on.

"I might have some news for you later. Did you have plans for tomorrow?"

Wyatt picked out a red T-shirt emblazoned with the baseball Cardinals' logo and slipped it on before picking the phone up again. "I don't know yet. What kind of news?"

"A meet and greet with some of the patrons from the Art Museum."

Wyatt made a face. He hated that sort of thing and Lukas knew it.

"It's good for your career." Same thing Lukas always said. Of course, he was right and Wyatt knew it. Didn't mean he had to like it.

"I know. All right. Whatever. Just let me know."

"Don't whatever me, boy."

Wyatt heard the chuckle in Lukas's voice, and knew he didn't mean anything by it.

"Tell you what. I was thinking of stopping by and checking on Shylor. How about I do that and then come over and let you know how he's doing, okay? I know you must be worried about him and all."

Wyatt made no immediate response.

"Wyatt?"

"Yeah, I'm here. I don't think that'll be necessary, you know?"

He exited the bedroom, barefoot, and headed downstairs, taking the stairs two at a time. There was a moment of silence from the other end of the line before Lukas growled in exasperation. "Oh dear God."

Wyatt had already reached the kitchen. He flinched at what he perceived as censure in Lukas's tone, but perhaps he was reading too much into it.

"You're going to get that boy hurt, do you realize that? Is that worth whatever's going on between you two?"

Wyatt shifted the phone to his left hand as he opened the fridge and pulled out the Tupperware with the leftover cinnamon rolls. He bumped the door closed with his ass and set the container on the counter.

"He's not a boy! And for your information, *he* came to *me*. He made the choice himself. No one forced him into it. Not Grant, not you, and certainly not me. I think that has to count for something." Wyatt lowered his voice to a low snarl, even though he knew there was no way he could be overheard, not by Shy. "You know something, Lukas? Shy's a grown man, and he deserves to be treated with respect. Not like Grant's personal slave. You do know that's illegal here, right? Ever hear of basic human rights?"

"That's not your call to make."

"No, it's not, it's his. I don't think he's ever been given a choice, Lukas. He was just stuck in a bad situation and left to rot. Why are you being such an ass?"

"Wyatt—"

"No, don't Wyatt me, Lukas. You're not much better, turning a blind eye to something you had to know was wrong. What does that make you, if not a silent accessory?" Not waiting for a reply, he ended the conversation, too angry to continue. He expected Lukas to phone right back, to pick up the argument where he'd dropped it, but that didn't happen. He wondered if he'd just screwed himself out of a mentor.

Couldn't worry about that now. Today was going to be all about Shy. The rest could wait.

CHAPTER TWELVE

ONE GOOD thing about Wyatt's anger at Lukas—it served to dampen his raging libido rather handily. He pounded angrily up the stairs, taking his frustration out on the innocent steps, holding inside the scream that threatened to tear itself loose. He paused at the top and forced himself to calm down. Losing control would do no one any good.

Taking a deep breath, he entered his bedroom and rummaged through the drawers until he found fresh clothes, which he laid out on the bed for Shy. The thought occurred to him that maybe they should go across the street and get some of Shy's own clothes. That might make him feel more comfortable. On the other hand, Wyatt wasn't sure he actually wanted to enter the house where Shylor had suffered abuse at the hands of the Keeper, much less take Shy back there.

Scratch that. They weren't going over there today. Or any other day, if Wyatt had anything to say about it. Maybe when Shy was ready to move out permanently, and then only if he had belongings he actually wanted to get back. And at a time when Grant wasn't there. As far as Wyatt was concerned, Shy's relationship with Randy Grant was over.

Wyatt paused just outside the bathroom door, listening to the steady rhythm of the water. He burned with the knowledge that Shy was standing underneath the spray, naked. Temptation pulled at him, the desire to touch Shy a growing ache in his soul.

Resolutely, he forced himself to push such thoughts away and hurried back to the relative safety of the kitchen.

Wyatt waited until Shy's footsteps sounded on the stairs before he set the container with the rolls into the microwave to warm for a few seconds. He poured a cup of coffee for each of them. Not sure how Shy took his, he'd set sweetener, sugar, honey, and liquid

138

creamer within easy reach. Removing the rolls, he set one on a small plate, which he placed next to Shy's mug. He raised his head at Shy's entrance.

The hot water had obviously agreed with him. His cheeks were flush with actual color, and his beautiful blue eyes held a little sparkle. He'd found the jeans and T-shirt Wyatt had laid out for him, but had forgone the shoes. Wouldn't matter if they didn't go out, anyhow. Wyatt preferred to be barefoot himself.

Shy slid into the chair opposite Wyatt's. Wyatt took a couple of rolls for himself and set the remainder on the table, in case Shy wanted more, then took his seat.

"Feel better?"

Shy nodded. He examined the various items Wyatt had laid out before him, as though he couldn't believe he could actually make his own choice. "Is the sweetener as sweet as the sugar?" he asked thoughtfully.

"Sweeter," Wyatt assured him. Shy's hand snaked out toward the honey, but at the last moment snatched a pink packet instead, tore it open, and stirred it into his coffee.

I know he can think for himself. He just needs to get away from that asshole.

"Want to try some of that creamer?" Wyatt offered. "It's cinnamon. My favorite."

That brought a definite smile to Shy's lips, and he took less time to make up his mind, closing his hand around the bottle and adding it to his cup. He stirred that in as well, then took a hesitant sip. Then a longer one. The smile of contentment that crossed over Shy's face warmed Wyatt's heart.

"You know what's really good?" Wyatt asked. Shy cocked an eyebrow in response.

"This." He broke off a piece of his cinnamon roll and dipped it into his coffee, just enough to wet it, then popped it into his mouth. He loved to dunk his pastries like this.

Shy hesitated for just a moment, then imitated Wyatt's actions, taking a piece of roll, giving it a quick coffee bath, and taking it into his mouth. His eyes grew wider as he chewed and swallowed.

"That *is* really good," he agreed. "Thanks for the suggestion."

They ate their breakfast in a companionable silence. Wyatt watched Shy carefully, although he couldn't have said just what he was looking for. When Shy finished his roll, he gave the container a wistful glance. Wyatt started to urge him to take another, then swallowed the words.

Let him make up his own mind. It's time he was allowed to think for himself.

After another minute or so of hesitation, Shy finally reached out and took a second roll. Wyatt couldn't help but feel that this was a small, but important, victory for Shy.

Once they'd finished eating, Shy stood and started to clear everything, but Wyatt insisted on helping, and the kitchen was clean again in no time.

I could get used to this.

Wyatt was surprised at his own thought. Not like he'd never lived with someone before. He had his college roommates, and he liked them well enough. But that was a temporary arrangement, born of necessity. Chances were once they all graduated, they'd fade out of one another's lives.

This was different. This was him and Shylor, and this was domestic, and he felt a surprising warmth he'd never known before. Wasn't it too soon to feel that way? Seriously, they barely knew each other. They came from completely different backgrounds and mind-sets. From what little Wyatt had learned so far, Shy had experienced horrors he could not even imagine. But it wasn't his suffering that drew Wyatt to him, it was his strength. His inner beauty. Something inside of the other young man called to something in himself, something basic and fundamental. He wanted nothing more than the chance to get to know Shy better, to find out what made him tick.

And most of all, he wanted to get Shy away from Randy Grant. He'd rather see him with someone else—*any*one else other than Grant.

"If I'm keeping you from something, I'll just go." Shy's voice broke into Wyatt's thoughts. Shy stood uncertainly in the middle of the kitchen. His gaze strayed about the room, as if seeking something else to clean, but everything was immaculate.

Wyatt's heart ached for him. Why did he always need to feel he had to be useful simply to exist? But he knew the answer to that question, didn't he? Randy Grant, damn his soul. That man would have much to account for some day, supposing there was an actual day of reckoning.

"You're not, don't even think that way," Wyatt replied. "I'm between classes right now. My time's my own."

"Aren't you working on… you know, art?" Shy waved vaguely in the direction of the back of the house and Wyatt's temporary studio.

"Yeah, but that's not for school." Shy's eyebrows raised curiously, so Wyatt hastened to explain. "I'm building up my portfolio. Lukas is working on getting me a show. Well, that's the plan anyway." He laughed, a little self-deprecatingly. *Starving artist* wasn't just an expression, it was a reality. Making it in the arts was difficult, at best. And talent was no guarantee of success. Sometimes it was all in the timing. Or who you knew.

"You'll do well, you're very talented."

Shy's words warmed Wyatt's heart.

"If you want to work, you know… I can just sit and watch. I mean, if you don't mind."

Wyatt hesitated. "I'm afraid you'll be bored," he halfheartedly protested.

"I won't be," Shy insisted.

Wyatt turned the suggestion over in his mind. Actually, he had something else in mind, an idea he'd been loath to broach before, unsure of Shy's reception. Maybe this was the perfect opportunity….

"Penny for your thoughts."

Wyatt hadn't realized he'd fallen silent until he heard the question, mimicking his own of that morning, Shy's tone light and teasing. Shy was actually smiling at him, which emboldened Wyatt all the more.

"Would you please sit for me?" Wyatt asked. "Let me paint your picture?"

"You want to paint *me*?" Shy sounded surprised. "Why?"

"Because you're beautiful," Wyatt blurted out without thinking.

Shy's face quickly pinked, but he didn't seem upset at the comment. At least, Wyatt hoped he wasn't. He seemed to be more skeptical than anything.

"You're too kind," Shy murmured. "There are far better subjects than me. I'd hate to see you waste your time—"

"I won't be, I promise. And we can talk while I work."

"Talk?" Shy sounded uncertain. "What about?"

"Anything. Everything. Nothing in particular." Wyatt tried to keep his voice at a reassuring level. He just wanted to get to know Shy, but nothing he would be uncomfortable in revealing. His likes and dislikes. His dreams and ambitions. That sort of thing. He wanted to give Shy the chance to know him better as well. Assuming he was interested, which was a huge assumption on his part.

Shy didn't say anything, and Wyatt's heart sank. He hoped he hadn't upset him. Sure, he wanted to paint him, but if Shy said no, he'd be fine with it. He might still be able to draw him from memory, if that was his only option. He started to tell him so, but Shy spoke first.

"All right," he said softly. "I'm all yours."

Wyatt's breath hitched at the words, although he knew they weren't meant the way he wanted to take them. Still, it was a start.

They refreshed their coffee cups and carried them to the back porch where Wyatt had his stuff set up.

"Aren't you going to wear a smock or something?" Shy asked. He was leafing through some of Wyatt's sketches on one of the glass-topped wicker tables in the room. Touching them gingerly, as if he was afraid to damage them.

"A smock?"

"You know, to paint in. I've seen pictures of artists wearing smocks. I just wondered."

Wyatt hid his smile once he realized Shy was being quite serious. "I'm not actually painting today. I have to sketch you first, before I even think about mixing a palette."

"Oh, okay." Shy seemed satisfied with his answer. "How did you want to paint me? What should I wear?"

There was that anxious look again. Wyatt hated to see him distressed for any reason. He hadn't thought beyond the question of asking Shy to pose, much less formulated any actual plan of action, such as where or what or how.

"Do you want me... to take my clothes off?" Shy's eyes were fixed on the floor, and his body had tensed suddenly. Much as Wyatt wanted to paint him au naturel, he wouldn't risk making Shy uncomfortable in order to do it. Maybe that would be a painful reminder of the times he'd been forced to put himself on display for the assholes at Randy's club. Lukas's club too, he reminded himself. Did that mean Lukas had seen Shy naked? He pushed the jealous thought aside, focusing on Shy. On the here and now.

Maybe it was time they got certain things out in the open. "Shy, sit down, please." He waved him toward the sofa. Shy hesitated for only a moment before doing as Wyatt requested. His fidgeting hands, which writhed in his lap, betrayed his uncertainty.

Wyatt started to pace the room, but stopped abruptly and dropped to his knees in front of Shy, putting them on a more even level. He carefully refrained from touching him, though, Lukas's admonition still ringing in his ears.

"Shy, I like you. I like you very much. I have ever since the first time I saw you, when you were washing—" He grew momentarily tongue-tied. He wasn't about to say that man's name if he could help it, so he slipped over it. "—the car," he hastily amended. "I wanted to get to know you, find out more about you. I'd be lying if I said I didn't think you're very attractive and very sexy, but there's more to you than that, and that's the part I want to get to know. I want to be your friend, if you'll have me."

Suddenly shy, and unexpectedly exposed, Wyatt paused for breath. He'd never bared his soul like this before, was surprised he even had it in him. He dropped his gaze to the floor, feeling rather foolish for being down on his knees like this, but unwilling to move away from Shy. Not yet. He hoped he hadn't screwed himself with Shy. He'd just wanted to be honest with him.

"I'd like that," Shy said so softly Wyatt could barely hear him. "I wanted the same thing when I saw you too."

Wyatt slowly raised his eyes to find Shy's gaze fixed intently on him.

"Friends," Wyatt repeated, and was gratified at Shy's nod.

"You aren't obligated to me for anything," Wyatt continued, feeling emboldened by Shy's acceptance, at least so far. "I won't ask you to do anything you don't want to do. Ever. If you don't want to, then you just say no. Okay?"

Shy nodded again.

"As for your question…. Maybe someday, when you're ready, I'll be more than happy to paint you in the nude. I think you'd make a great model. But only if that's something you'd feel comfortable with. Right now, I want you just the way you are. Does that make sense?"

Shy hesitated for a moment, then nodded. A wave of relief washed over Wyatt.

"Would you like me to do something?" Shy asked.

Wyatt was momentarily confused by the question. "What do you mean?"

"I dunno." Shy shrugged. "I thought maybe you'd want me to pose a certain way, so it's not just me sitting here looking stupid."

Good question. Most of Wyatt's experience with drawing live models came from his classes, where he had no choice of what pose the model assumed. This was another matter entirely.

Wyatt glanced around the room. He could get a piece of fruit out of the kitchen, but that sounded like a stupid idea as soon as he thought it. Most painting poses were stiff and unnatural in Wyatt's eyes. Then he remembered something they'd done together the first night Shy had slept here.

"You want to read while I paint?" Brilliant idea. It would make for a relaxed pose, and maybe even get Shy to relax himself, if he was caught up in the book.

"I like that idea," Shy admitted.

"How about Alice?" Wyatt suggested. He was gratified to see the smile that lit Shy's face. When Shy started to rise, Wyatt stopped him, placing his hands on his knees. Shy stilled instantly.

Cursing himself inwardly for his mistake, Wyatt hurriedly removed the offending hands and rose, as if nothing had happened. "I know where it is. Drink your coffee, I'll be right back." He winked at Shy, hoping to set him at ease, and hastily left the room. The book sat where they'd left it. He snatched it up and brought it quickly back.

"Did you want to put your feet up and read?" Wyatt suggested. "Kind of relax?"

"If that's how you want me," Shy acquiesced.

Wyatt resisted the urge to remind Shy that he wasn't Randy and Shy did have a choice in the matter. *Not too fast,* he cautioned himself. *Take it easy.*

"Let's try that and see how it goes." He glanced around the room. Selecting a wicker chair, he placed it across from the couch and sat in it. Dissatisfied, he pushed it back until he found the perfect distance. He picked up his sketch pad and pencil, and began to draw.

CHAPTER THIRTEEN

EVEN THOUGH they hadn't set an alarm, Shy woke early the next morning. Some habits were too hard to break. But for once he didn't feel an overwhelming compulsion to leap out of bed. Instead, he rolled over, maintaining a cautious distance from Wyatt, and quietly watched him sleep. There was something comforting in the gentle rise and fall of the other man's chest, the occasional flutter of his closed eyes. The way he randomly smiled to himself, as though he were having a very pleasant dream. Shy envied him that. Shy seldom remembered his dreams. And most of the dreams he did recall were painful ones. That was one reason why he disliked sleeping any longer than necessary.

Giving in to an urge he couldn't explain, Shy edged a little closer. But Wyatt never stirred. He must be very tired. Not surprising. They'd spent a long afternoon in the art room, as Wyatt worked, followed by a longer night playing video games.

Wyatt had spent hours sketching Shy to his satisfaction. At first nothing seemed to please him. He wadded up sketch after sketch and tossed it to the floor, then started on another. After a while, the floor had become a minefield of discarded efforts.

Shy didn't mind. Wyatt's passion for his craft was evident in every move he made, the way he clutched his pencil as he drew, the steely determination in his eye, the slight crease of his forehead, puckered in concentration. And when he glanced between his sketchbook and Shy…. Shy found himself deluged with feelings he couldn't explain. Heady sensations coursed through him such as he'd never experienced before. Wyatt looked at him as if he saw something in him no one else ever had. Something worthwhile, not damaged goods.

After a while, Wyatt had set the sketch aside, saying something about it being a good start as he rose and stretched his back, with a loud pop. Then he apologized profusely for not even giving Shy a break, although Shy kept telling him he was fine. To make amends, Wyatt ordered in a pizza from a local parlor. They ate the pizza and washed it down with glasses of white wine, then played video games on the homeowner's huge TV, staying up until the wee hours of the morning.

Shy couldn't remember the last time he'd had so much fun.

The even cadence of Wyatt's breathing changed, probably a sign he was waking. Shy started to scoot back to his former position, but before he could put his plan into effect, Wyatt had rolled toward him, and now Shy was looking directly into those big blue eyes, and he couldn't have moved if he'd wanted to. Which he didn't.

"Morning," Wyatt greeted him. "You sleep good?"

"Yeah. You?"

"Beautifully."

Wyatt had a gorgeous smile. And kissable lips. Acting on impulse, Shy darted forward and kissed him softly. Shocked by his own boldness, he felt his cheeks go warm. He anxiously scanned Wyatt's face for a reaction. Wyatt seemed frozen in place, eyes wide.

"I'm sor—"

Before Shy could get out any more of his apology, Wyatt had stilled him with a gentle kiss. Soft, yet passionate without being rough. A kiss with a great deal of promise. Then another. And another. And then Shy stopped thinking at all.

Shy's head was spinning by the time Wyatt pulled back, regarding him with concerned eyes. He thought Wyatt murmured something that sounded like, "Too soon, too soon," but he couldn't be sure, and the next moment Wyatt excused himself and headed to the bathroom.

By the time he returned, Shy had made the bed, and was smoothing the blanket down. Temptation averted… for now.

"Let's go see what we can scare up for breakfast," Wyatt suggested.

"Don't you want to get dressed first?" Shy asked.

"Let's see how the day goes."

Shy followed Wyatt down the stairs and into the kitchen.

"You mind starting the coffee?" Wyatt asked as he rummaged through the refrigerator. "I think we have the makings of a decent omelet, and that's one thing I can cook. You like omelets?" He pulled his head out of the fridge to regard Shy.

"Yeah, I make them a lot, but I have to make them with whites only. The dietician insists." He shrugged. "They're healthier that way."

Wyatt snorted. He emerged from the fridge juggling a carton of eggs, a package of shredded cheese, and what looked to be fresh herbs. "Sorry, I don't do healthy. There's a reason eggs have yolks, you know. And it's not just to look pretty."

Shy giggled at Wyatt's silliness. He dumped the grounds from the day before and added a fresh filter, followed by coffee from the can. He filled the carafe with water and emptied it into the coffee maker, then flipped a switch to start the brewing process. "There's juice left from yesterday, want me to pour some?" he offered.

"That would be great, thanks."

Shy got out two small glasses and set them on the table, then got out the pitcher he'd freshly squeezed the day before and poured it into the glasses and set it on the table. He took a seat and sipped at his while Wyatt whisked the eggs and poured them into a small skillet. Wyatt wore only a pair of sleep pants, which hung about his hips. He seemed to be very comfortable in his own skin. Shy took advantage of the fact Wyatt wore no shirt to stare at his nipples. They were larger than his own, darker. There was something very inviting about them. Shy found he couldn't draw his eyes from the sight.

When Wyatt's gaze caught his, Shy blushed and quickly shifted his attention back to his juice. Wyatt made no comment. Perhaps he hadn't noticed. And maybe that was wishful thinking on his part.

"What kind of herbs are those?" Shy asked.

"Tarragon," Wyatt replied. "You're not allergic, are you?"

"I don't think so."

"Good." Shy looked up, just in time to catch Wyatt's smile. "This won't take long. Omelets are good for fast breakfasts. Anyone can make 'em, even me." He laughed as he added the cheese, then folded the mixture in the pan over, waited a moment, then plated it before starting on the second omelet.

"I think the coffee's done," Shy murmured. "I'll pour." He needed to do something other than stare at Wyatt's half-naked body. That couldn't end well. Quickly rising, he got two mugs from the cabinet, and creamer from the refrigerator, and prepared their coffees the way Wyatt had the day before, then took his seat once more.

"Wish we had some bacon," Wyatt commented. He flipped off the burner and pushed the pan back, sprinkled tarragon over the omelets, and lifted both plates. "Maybe next time. I know I need to go to the store, but I should probably call Lukas first, see if he's still talking to me, before I start making any plans—" A stricken look crossed Wyatt's face, as if he'd said something he shouldn't. He quickly set one of the plates in front of Shy, then laid the second at his own place and sat down.

"What do you mean?" Shy asked, frowning. "Why wouldn't Lukas be talking to you?"

Wyatt had stuffed a bite of omelet into his mouth and couldn't speak immediately. Was that deliberate? When he'd finished and washed it down with first juice, then coffee, he took a deep breath and finally addressed Shy. "I didn't mean it like that. I'm sure he's speaking to me," he hastily amended. "That's an exaggeration, you know? He doesn't like the way I try to blow off these little parties he gets me invited to. I know they're for my own good, but, well…." He shrugged. "I'll call him when we're done here. There's supposed to be a get-together this afternoon. I have to say, they do feed you pretty good at those things." He forced a smile, but Shy got the distinct feeling there was something Wyatt wasn't telling him.

"What kind of a party is it?" Shy asked.

"We call them meet and greets," Wyatt said. "The artists get together with the patrons, mingle, schmooze, that kind of thing. Discuss our work, our visions. Our artistic dreams. In other words, we have to look our best so someone will want to sponsor us."

"That doesn't sound too bad," Shy commented.

"You wouldn't think so, would you? It's not that simple. How's your omelet?"

"Delicious," Shy assured him.

They concentrated on eating for a few minutes. Shy could sense Wyatt was turning something over in his mind. He could see it in his eyes. He just didn't know what that something was.

Suddenly Wyatt snapped his fingers, and Shy jumped a little.

"I have an idea."

"What's that?" Shy asked, curious to know what had piqued Wyatt's interest.

"If I remember correctly, this thing's going to be held near the Art Museum. How about we stop in there for a few minutes?"

"The Art Museum?" Shy couldn't believe what he was hearing. "I've never been there." He raised his mug to his lips, watching Wyatt over the brim.

Wyatt looked aghast. "You've *never* been?"

There were a lot of places in St. Louis Shy had never been, thanks to Randy. And the places he'd been he didn't want to discuss.

Why did he have to think of Randy now? The very thought of the older man was enough to make him lose his appetite. He pushed his plate back and rose, but before he could even think about rushing out of the room, Wyatt had risen and come around the table.

"It's okay, it's okay." He pulled Shy into a quick embrace. "We can fix that, it's easy. We only have time for a short visit today, but we can come back later, when we aren't pushed for time. There's so much there I'd love to show you."

Shy knew he should say no, knew he should face the reality of his situation. He was Randy's to do with as he pleased, and Randy would not like this. Not at all.

A little voice in the back of his head whispered that Randy didn't have to know. Who was going to tell him? Certainly not Wyatt. *Make the most of this, for as long as it lasts.*

Wyatt's arms were strong, his chest comfortable. Shy gave in and rested against him, breathing him in. He wished this moment would never end. But of course it did.

He drew back finally and met Wyatt's concerned gaze. "Okay," he said. "If you want me to go with you. I don't think I have anything really nice to wear, though."

"That doesn't matter. This is informal. We'll find something for both of us to wear." Wyatt's smile was radiant now, and Shy felt himself relax a little.

"Are you going to call Lukas?"

"Actually, I'll just text him and ask for the address. That way I won't have to write it down." As he spoke, Wyatt took his phone out and began to type with both thumbs. Satisfied with his message, he replaced the phone in his pocket. Why did Shy get the impression he was avoiding a confrontation of some kind?

"Why don't we finish eating and get dressed?" Wyatt suggested. He brushed his thumb across Shy's cheekbone softly.

"Okay," Shy agreed, leaning into Wyatt's touch.

I'm in so much trouble.

CHAPTER FOURTEEN

TEXTING LUKAS instead of calling him was avoidance on Wyatt's part, and he knew it. But he didn't want to continue the argument with his mentor and chance Shy overhearing anything he shouldn't. Things were going too well to fuck them up now. Shy was definitely warming to him and relaxing more. He wasn't nearly as tense as when he'd first arrived, the night of Grant's heart attack.

Touched that Shy had sought him out in his time of need, Wyatt had only wanted to protect him. But he couldn't deny there was something between them, something palpable. And Wyatt intended to fan that spark until it had a chance to grow into a flame. He wasn't sure where their relationship might go, but he definitely wanted to find out.

But first he had to figure out how to get—and keep—Shy away from Randy Grant.

There was no telling when the man would be released from the hospital. Maybe as early as Monday. Wyatt was surprised he hadn't phoned Shy even once the day before, or demanded Lukas bring him up to see him again. But maybe Grant realized even he didn't exactly look his best in a hospital gown, with his ass hanging out, and maybe his vanity overrode other considerations. Frankly, he didn't know how that man's warped mind worked.

Still, time had to be drawing short, and something needed to be done. Wyatt's natural inclination was to keep Shy safe with him, there at Masterson's house, but that might be too close for comfort for Shy. Right now, though, he didn't have any alternate suggestions. And he didn't think he could discuss the matter with Lukas, not in his current mood.

Wyatt was half afraid Lukas would call him in response to his message. But his fears were put to rest a few minutes later, as they were getting dressed, when Lukas texted the time and location of this afternoon's event. The address belonged to one of those big old three-story houses on Lindell, the kind that even put this neighborhood to shame. Lukas already had some of Wyatt's art with him, including the piece he'd finished in the middle of the night and messengered to him via an Uber driver who was a fellow art student as well as a friend. Wyatt's paintings would be displayed, along with that of other starving artists who were also vying for recognition, in the hopes of attracting a patron or two. Backing was everything in the art world, every artist vied for it. There was no mention of anything that had passed between the two of them earlier, for which Wyatt was grateful.

"Is that from Lukas?"

He looked up from the phone screen to find Shy had found a warm blue button-down shirt of Masterson's that fit, along with a pair of dark dress slacks that nicely accentuated his slender build. His pale blond hair hung loose about his shoulders, and the total effect stunned Wyatt into momentary silence. "Wow, you look really good," he managed to get out finally, as Shy blushed. "Oh, sorry. Yeah, Lukas texted the address. We'll have just enough time for me to show you want I wanted you to see at the Museum and then head over. It isn't far."

Shy nodded, his gaze raking Wyatt up and down. "You always look good," he said simply, not that Wyatt had asked, and now it was Wyatt's turn to blush.

"Is there anything you need to take with you?" Shy asked, thankfully diverting Wyatt's attention.

"Just us. Lukas will take care of the rest." Of course, he hadn't actually told Lukas he was bringing Shy, but if the man had half a brain, he'd surely figure it out, especially once he got the new painting. If not, he'd realize it soon enough when they showed up together.

Making their way to the front door, Wyatt ushered Shy out, then closed and locked the house behind them. Masterson's luxury sedan sat waiting in the drive where he'd parked it. Wyatt opened the passenger door for Shy before quickly rounding the car, taking his place behind the wheel. He noticed Shy never once glanced toward the house across the street. That was a good sign, surely?

Traffic on Skinker Boulevard was reasonably light and Wyatt made good time. Soon they'd made the turn onto Lagoon, passing into Forest Park. Wyatt loved the tree-filled park. It was a beautiful little haven in the middle of the city. He wished they had more time to properly explore the area. They would someday, he vowed. He'd do his best to make up for everything Shy had been denied before, as much as he possibly could. Wyatt didn't have a great deal of money, but there were a lot of things to do and see in St. Louis that didn't cost an arm and a leg—in fact, many were free—and a number of them were to be found in Forest Park.

He turned onto Fine Arts Drive, heading up the hill to the familiar building which graced the top of the rise. Once known as the Palace of Fine Arts, it was originally constructed for the 1904 World's Fair, and was the only structure still remaining from that time. Parking at the Art Museum could be a bit tricky at times. Those who could afford it anted up the fifteen dollars to park in the newly built garage, which directly adjoined the building. Those on a budget, like Wyatt, jockeyed for position in the free lots nearby.

Turning into one of the small parking areas, Wyatt almost didn't spot the brake lights of a red minivan. The question was—was it coming or going? He quickly braked, watching for some sort of indication. Luck was with them, and the driver was pulling out. Wyatt quickly zipped into the vehicle's vacated space before anyone else could lay claim to the spot, and gave a fist pump of triumph once he'd parked. "Yes!" His action produced laughter from Shy. The sound was music to Wyatt's ears.

"You know what, before we go in, let's pay our respects to Louis." Wyatt turned to Shy with a wink and a grin.

"Louis who?" Shy wanted to know.

"I'll introduce you," Wyatt said mysteriously as they exited the car. He led Shy up to a huge statue on a concrete viewing platform across from the entrance to the museum. They stood at the base, looking up at the large bronze figure. "Shy, meet his majesty, King Louis IX. The man St. Louis is named after."

"Wow," Shy said as he gazed up at the man and his steed. "I didn't know we were named after anyone. Guess I never thought about it much."

"I read something somewhere that it's because he's the only French king to be made a saint, and the first settlers were French, so I guess that was important to them."

"That makes sense," Shy replied.

After a few minutes of paying their respects to the long dead monarch, Wyatt led Shy to the end of the platform away from the museum. "Check out this view," he said. "That's Art Hill, right below us. Down there's the Grand Basin. This was all part of the World's Fair, back in 1904. I bet it was really something to see. I read that the Ferris wheel was so large, they could fit like fifty people in every car. And there was a hell of a view when you got to the top."

"Wow," Shy repeated. "I can't even imagine that." They stood in silent awe, taking in the verdant vista before them. Wyatt always stopped to pay his respects to the French king whenever he came to the museum, as well as take in the scenic view afforded by the lookout. Too bad they didn't have time to do much more than that today. Reluctantly, he turned Shy away from the park and toward the museum, across Fine Arts Drive, up the steps, and inside. Not stopping to ask for directions, he veered left into a large gallery, then left again into a smaller room. Ignoring the paintings and sculpture they passed, he headed straight into the next gallery, number 218, which was their destination. There was the painting he'd wanted to share with Shy. Monet's *Water Lilies.*

The large painting hung in solitary splendor on one wall. The two young men stood in respectful silence before it, taking in the sheer beauty of Monet's masterpiece. Over six feet in length, the delicate blossoms bloomed in watery splendor, a veritable sea of blues and greens.

"That's beautiful," Shy murmured. He stepped closer and placed his hand inside Wyatt's. Wyatt gently closed his hand around Shy's, his heart skipping a beat at his action, as well as his proximity. If they had more time, he would have proposed they sit on the low bench situated just behind them, one of many scattered about the museum. Look at the painting and simply be together. But unfortunately they had somewhere else to be.

"There's about two hundred fifty of these water lily paintings by Monet, all around the world," Wyatt said. "I just love Monet. All the Impressionists, actually. They did such beautiful work."

"*You* do beautiful work," Shy said, squeezing Wyatt's hand.

"Thank you," Wyatt replied, warmed by Shy's touch.

"Someday," Shy said, turning toward Wyatt with a grin, "when your paintings are hanging here, I'll be able to tell people I knew you when. Assuming you aren't too famous to talk to me then."

"I'll never be that famous," Wyatt said quickly.

They swayed toward one another, as if mesmerized, and Wyatt thought he saw Shy's lips part expectantly. And he wanted to kiss him, yes he did. But the buzzing of his cell phone broke the moment. Incoming text, three guesses who from. Wyatt glanced at the screen. Yep, Lukas.

"Guess we better get going," he said reluctantly. "Lukas is already there. But I'll bring you back here another time, I promise. And we'll spend as long as we want, just looking around. And we'll do lunch too. Someplace special. Maybe Blueberry Hill."

"That sounds good. I'd like that." Shy's warm smile was reward enough for Wyatt.

Looking into Shy's beautiful sky-blue eyes, Wyatt came to a sudden realization. He was in love with Shylor. Shy had become the world to him, and he'd do anything to keep him safe, no matter what. No matter who he had to tell to fuck off. He didn't care what Lukas said. Lukas didn't know everything, and he was wrong about the two of them.

They sky was just starting to cloud up when they returned to the car. He hoped it wouldn't rain until after they got back home. Good thing this was not an outdoor event.

Wyatt opened Shy's door for him again, but before Shy got in, he kissed Wyatt softly on the lips. "Thank you so much," he said. "For everything." He slid inside without waiting for a response. As Wyatt walked around the car, his smile surely stretched from ear to ear.

"We're not late, are we?" Shy asked as they drove the short distance to Lindell Boulevard.

"Nah, we're good. Most people show up fashionably late, as they like to put it." He chuckled. "Just an excuse for not being on time, if you ask me." Not that he had room to talk. Punctuality was not his strong suit.

Wyatt checked the address on his phone once more. Just a few blocks down. Well, at least they wouldn't look out of place in this neighborhood in Masterson's elegant ride.

Spotting empty curb space near their destination, Wyatt pulled over and parked. The street was tree-lined, and the elegant homes were a decent distance apart, not on top of each other as they tended to be farther into the city.

"It's just up there." He pointed. "We can walk the rest of the way."

The house they were looking for was even fancier than Wyatt had expected. A circular drive ran behind a large stone fountain adorned by water nymphs. Balustraded steps led to the entrance of the three-storied pale brick house. He wasn't sure he'd ever want a house this size to call his own. Of course, that was easy to say when he couldn't afford to rent even a small apartment.

The front door was opened by a tall middle-aged woman in a maid's uniform. She welcomed them with a warm smile, told them where the buffet was located, and where they would find the art that was being displayed, as well as the other guests, then wished them a good afternoon. They thanked her and entered the house.

Wyatt had to admit this was one of the nicer homes he'd been to for these affairs. Of course, he didn't attend them all, much to Lukas's chagrin. But he was coming to realize he needed to make an effort for the sake of his career. Talent alone wouldn't carry the day. He had to learn to schmooze if he wanted to get ahead. Having Shy with him today made the idea far more palatable than it had been before.

"You want to get something to eat? Check out the buffet and see what they have?" Wyatt asked.

"I'm not really hungry, are you?" Shy replied.

Wyatt shook his head.

"Maybe later?" Shy suggested. "I'd really like to take a look at your art first. That is, if you don't mind."

"I don't mind at all. I just hope you won't be disappointed."

In response, Shy looped his arm through Wyatt's and said softly, "I could never be disappointed in you." Wyatt warmed at the compliment.

A number of other people had arrived before them. A steady flow of guests moved from one room to another. Wyatt searched for any sign of Lukas, but he was nowhere in evidence. He did spot the friend who had Ubered the late-night delivery for him. Or rather Martin spotted him first, approaching with a big grin.

"How's it going?" Martin greeted him.

"Good, I guess. Just got here," Wyatt replied. "I was looking for Lukas. You seen him?"

"Yeah, he's in that direction." Martin jerked his chin down the hall. "I delivered your painting, by the way. I think he was a little less than thrilled, considering the lateness of the hour and all."

"I couldn't help it," Wyatt mumbled.

"I know. I think he understands, being an artist himself. You gotta go with it when that lightning strikes, right?" Martin laughed. Wyatt noticed him cast curious glances at Shy before Wyatt remembered his manners.

"Martin, this is Shylor. Shy, this is Martin. Fellow art student and Uber driver."

"Nice to meet you," Shy said.

"You as well," Martin replied. "You'll have to point out which painting I delivered for you, dude. I'm just curious to see what was so important it had to get there in the middle of the night."

"I will," Wyatt said. "Give us a chance to look around first." And maybe a chance to receive the rough side of Lukas's tongue, depending on what sort of mood his mentor was in. "Thanks again for your help. I appreciate it."

"No problem. What are bros for?" He held out one hand for a fist bump, which was reciprocated. "Catch up with you later, going to check out the food." He nodded at Shy before heading in the other direction. Wyatt and Shy continued down the hall toward the main event.

"What painting was he talking about?" Shy asked.

"The one I was working on yesterday."

"But how… I mean… so fast? Why?"

"I was just… I wanted to…." Wyatt tripped all over his words as he attempted to explain the compulsion that had driven him to complete the painting in the middle of the night, as Shy slept.

"You inspired me," he simply said at last. "I couldn't think of anything but finishing. I hope you don't mind that I sent it to Lukas for today. I mean, if you do, we'll take it down, no questions asked. I should have asked you first, I'm sorry."

Now it was Shy's turn to be flummoxed. "Um… I mean…. No, it's all right. I trust you. I just thought oils took a while."

They paused in the hall. Wyatt gently stroked Shy's cheek. "Thank you," he said. "Actually, they do. I used watercolors for this one. I want to do one in oil, later."

"Okay," Shy said. "Then I guess I need to see this, don't I?"

"Absolutely."

CHAPTER FIFTEEN

THE ROOM where they ended up was a good-sized interior room without windows, the sole illumination coming from recessed lighting in the ceiling. A number of people milled about. Clustered in small groups, they peered attentively at the artwork on the walls, as well as the sculptures set on a number of small tables scattered around the room, chatting amongst themselves. Shy drew closer to Wyatt, keeping a tight hold on his hand. He kept telling himself he'd be fine as long as he was with Wyatt. But he was seldom around this many people at one time, and their number and proximity was making him nervous.

"Are you okay?" Wyatt asked in a voice laced with concern. Just having him ask the question made Shy feel better. It felt good to have someone actually care how he felt.

"I'm fine," he assured him. As if to reinforce that thought, he squeezed Wyatt's hand. The smile he received in return was breathtaking. Shy's heart felt as though it was expanding inside his chest. Everyone around them receded into the background, and there was only Wyatt and him....

"Here he is." A familiar voice broke the illusion, and the moment passed. Shy looked up to find Lukas standing there, as well as some woman he didn't recognize. She was tall and thin, with short dark hair. One side of her head was shaved, and the simple black dress she wore did nothing to hide a number of tattoos spread over her arms and neck.

"Nicole, I'd like you to meet Wyatt Findley, the artist I was just telling you about." He glanced at Shy, as if seeing him for the first time, then quickly added, "And this is his friend, Shylor Lind. Gentlemen, this is Nicole Morgan. She's on the board at the Art Museum, as well as being a fellow art lover, and she's been kind enough to stop by and take a look at some of my students' work."

Nicole offered her hand, first to Wyatt, then to Shy. "Nice to meet you," she said. "Lukas has really been talking you up for some time, Wyatt. When he told me you'd be here today, I had to come see what the hoopla was about. Lukas doesn't brag about just anybody."

"I love that tattoo on your wrist," Shy blurted out without thinking. Shit, he shouldn't have spoken. That's the kind of thing Randy would punish him for.

Why did he have to think of him now? When everything was going so well without him? He braced himself for some sort of fallout.

Nicole didn't seem offended at his question. She turned her hand over so he could get a better view of the unusual spiral heart inked there. "Thank you," she said. "It's a copy of one Marilyn Manson designed. In case you can't tell, I'm a huge fan." An exact duplicate of the tattoo graced her other wrist.

Shy wasn't familiar with Manson, but if this was some of her art, she must be cool.

"Very nice," Wyatt said. "For a musician, he does some very interesting artwork. I've seen some of his stuff on the internet. A little too pricey for my pocketbook, though."

"I know the feeling," Nicole sympathized.

Shy was confused, but he didn't say anything. Wasn't Marilyn a woman's name? He'd have to ask Wyatt about that later.

"I've been looking at some of your work, Wyatt, and I have to agree with Lukas that you're a very talented artist. And I'm seen some very talented artists in my time."

"Thank you," Wyatt said. "I appreciate that. Lukas is a good mentor."

"I totally agree with you, Nicole," Lukas interjected. "This young man is going to go far, I think. Just needs a little help to get there."

Nicole looked thoughtfully back and forth between Wyatt and Shy. A smile bloomed on her lips. "You have a very lovely boyfriend, Wyatt. I can see where you draw your inspiration from."

Shy warmed at her words. Even more so when Wyatt didn't correct her assumption. Even if it wasn't true, the sentiment sounded nice, and fed into his inner fantasies.

"Yes I do," Wyatt said, sliding his arm around Shy's waist. Shy automatically drew closer, without hesitation. This felt too natural not to.

Did Wyatt really mean what he said, or was this a show he was putting on for a potential patron? He decided not to analyze it.

"I hate to do this, but I have another appointment this afternoon. But it was very nice to meet both of you." Nicole turned to Lukas. "Sorry I have to run already. Walk me to the door?"

"Of course," Lukas responded. He cast a quick glance toward Wyatt and Shy, but if he had any comment to make, he kept it to himself. They murmured their goodbyes to Nicole before she and Lukas left the room.

Wyatt lifted Shy's hand to his lips and kissed it softly. "I would like nothing more than to be your boyfriend, Shy. What do you think? Can we do that?"

Shy's heart felt as though it might beat out of his chest. *If this is a dream, please let it never end.*

He took a deep breath but, not trusting his voice, simply nodded. Wyatt kissed his hand again, before letting their twined grip fall back into place. "Let's find that painting and take a look at it," he said, drawing Shy carefully through the other guests in the direction Lukas and Nicole had come from.

Shy followed Wyatt blindly. He had eyes for no one and nothing but Wyatt at that moment. He didn't care about the other artists or their work. He felt as though his whole world revolved around Wyatt. He had never felt so happy before, or so loved. He had never believed anyone could truly love him. His own mother had sold him without a second thought to a man old enough to be his father. He couldn't even pretend she didn't know what was going to happen. She'd made that clear enough with her parting words. He was to obey Randy and do *every*thing he said to do.

As for Randy, he didn't love anyone but himself. If nothing else, Shy had learned that about the man over the past fifteen years. Everything he did was for his own pleasure, his own purpose. Shy was just another belonging to him, bought and paid for. His own personal slave, to be used and abused.

But Wyatt…. Wyatt saw Shy as a person. He asked for nothing, certainly demanded nothing. He didn't want to use him sexually—he saw them as equals. He looked out for him, made him feel safe. Shy wanted to stay with Wyatt for as long as he could. Was it possible… did they have a future together? He hoped so with his whole heart.

Lost in thought, he was surprised when they stopped suddenly. Oh yeah, the painting. It hung near a corner of the room, with some of Wyatt's other art. A few people were oohing and aahing over it. They waited until the others had moved on before stepping closer.

Shy was immediately overwhelmed with emotion as he stared at Wyatt's flattering depiction of himself. He wasn't sure what he'd been expecting. Certainly not to look as good as Wyatt had made him. The colors in the background were muted, as though the room was in shadow, the foreground highlighting Shy as he read.

"Wow," he said. Anything else seemed inadequate, although that single word was far from eloquent. He looked up at Wyatt. Why did he look so anxious?

"Do you really like it?"

Shy threw his arms around Wyatt and hugged him. "I love it," he said. "I love *you*."

It took a moment for Shy to realize the words that had slipped out of his mouth. Eyes wide, he tried to draw back, thinking maybe he needed to run, but Wyatt gently held him in place. Shy risked a look at Wyatt's face. Wyatt looked astounded. Shy couldn't tell if it was happiness or horror he was witnessing. And he was afraid to find out.

The next moment, his fears were allayed when Wyatt kissed him. Shy melted into the kiss, their arms naturally wrapping about each other. Wyatt's lips were warm and soft… and dare he think it, loving? By the time they came up for air, Shy felt light-headed, but good.

"I love you too," Wyatt whispered.

Shy felt as though he might cry. So many emotions swirling through him. Feelings he'd never experienced before. Suddenly, he didn't want to be here. He wanted to be alone with Wyatt. Away from everyone in a world of their own.

"Let's get out of here," Wyatt said, as though he'd read Shy's mind. "What do you say?"

Before Shy had a chance to respond, they were interrupted by a figure hurrying toward them—Lukas had returned. He tried not to frown, even though he knew Lukas would undoubtedly want Wyatt to stay longer, talk to more people. He probably would tell them they couldn't leave yet. But looking at Lukas, he saw something in the man's demeanor that scared him.

"Wyatt, you have to get him out of here. *Right* now."

Wyatt looked as confused as Shy felt. Surely Lukas wasn't mad that they kissed, assuming he'd seen that? Or was he? His next words dispelled that theory.

"Randy's here, no time to explain, just go! *Now!*"

Wyatt took Shy's hand and turned him toward the door. Shy was too much in shock to argue. How had this even happened?

"Why am I not surprised to find you here? With *him*?"

Too late. Shy knew that voice too well to pretend otherwise. The fact that he wasn't yelling, that he seemed to be calm and controlled, made it all the more likely Randy Grant was seething inside. Shy cast an apprehensive glance at Randy, too frightened to speak.

Randy's face was a cold mask as he glanced between Shy and Wyatt, who'd wound his arms protectively around Shy.

If not for Wyatt's arms bracing him, Shy would have surely fallen.

I'm going to die....

WYATT ACTED without thinking. Every instinct he had told him to hold on to Shy for dear life, to protect him from Randy Grant. How the man even came to be there when he should by rights have still been in the hospital was immaterial—he was there now, and damned if Wyatt was going to let him get his hands on Shy again, much less hurt him.

He'd suspected this encounter would have to happen at some point, this showdown with the obnoxious older man. But he hadn't expected it to be today of all days. And certainly not here. Right this minute, he wanted nothing more than to smash his fist into Grant's face. Cause him pain, although nothing like what he'd probably inflicted on Shy over the years. His first consideration was for Shy. He needed to take care of him before anything else.

Shy trembled in Wyatt's arms, and his heart ached for him. What a terrible position to be in. He wanted to take him away from here immediately, but somehow he knew with Grant here, that wouldn't be so easy. Wyatt tightened his grip, trying to convey his reassurance to Shy that he was safe, he wouldn't let Grant have him.

Grant's lip curled up into an ugly sneer, his gaze fixed on Wyatt and Shy. He took a step toward them, but Lukas quickly stepped between them.

"Randy, I'm surprised to see you here. I didn't think they'd let you out so soon. How are you doing? Do you want to sit down somewhere? Maybe we can get a drink?"

If anything, Lukas's intervention had the opposite effect of what was intended. Wyatt guessed that it was the inference that he was some kind of a weakling who should be under a doctor's care.

"I'm here because I signed myself out," he snarled, still in a low voice. Although something about the situation was beginning to draw the attention of others in the room. Perhaps it was the combative posturing that was going on. "I had to call a cab to get home. Imagine my surprise when I couldn't get any answer on the house phone." He glared at Shy, who remained silent, shrinking back against Wyatt.

Grant attempted to step around Lukas, but Wyatt's mentor kept blocking him. Grant gave up, at least for the moment, meeting Wyatt's defiant gaze, his own eyes narrowed. "I knew you were trouble the first time I saw you. I should have taken care of you then and there. When I got home and realized Shy wasn't there, I walked across the street and noticed you were gone too. So I made a few calls, put two and two together, and here I am."

"Well, all's well that ends well. Have you seen the buffet? They have quite the layout. I'm sure you could use some better food than what you've been getting." Lukas laid his hand on the other man's arm, as if he intended to steer him away from the conflict, but Grant shook him off.

"Forget it. I don't have time for this shit. I want to go home." He pointed at Shy with an imperious gesture. "Come with me. *Now*. I will *deal* with you when we get home."

Wyatt felt Shy's entire body begin to quiver in his grasp. Damn that Randy Grant all to hell, he had no right to do this. None at all.

"Forget it, Grant," Wyatt spoke up for the first time. He released Shy just long enough to move him protectively behind him. Shy wound his arms around Wyatt's waist, his head buried against Wyatt's back. "He's not going anywhere with you. Not now, not ever. You don't own him, and never have."

"I'm not talking to *you*, I'm talking to Shylor. He knows who I am to him, even if you don't, and don't ever doubt he will always obey me. So kindly remove your hands from him now. You will have no contact with him in any way. And do not *ever* come near either one of us again." He glanced at Lukas. "You need to explain to your boy there the sad bad facts of life, and remove those rose-tinted glasses he's wearing. Time he learned how the real world works."

Wyatt wanted to pounce on Grant and beat him to a pulp, but he knew violence would solve nothing. As if reading his mind, Lukas said, "Just hold on there, Wyatt, let me handle this."

"There's nothing to handle, Lukas," Grant said. "Just stand aside and we'll be going. Shy, to me. *Now.*"

"No. Shy, don't move. Randy, stop," Lukas continued. "You have no right to come in here and talk to him like that. None at all."

Grant snorted. Wyatt was surprised at how unruffled he seemed. Maybe the doctors had put him on some kickass drugs before he checked himself out. Hopefully whatever it was would keep him docile long enough for Shy and him to make their exit.

"You know what right I have. Are you going to dare to stand there and lecture me on my lifestyle when you're no better yourself? Are you going to play the hypocrite, or should I remind you of some of the subs I've seen you with over the years? The things I've seen you do to them?"

"Having a sub is one thing, and yeah, I'm not ashamed to admit it." Lukas drew himself up to his full height, staring Grant down. "But this? This is not that. What you have with Shy... that's just wrong. You don't know the first thing about being a Dom. It's not just laying down the law and proving who's the boss. It's caring for someone else totally and completely. You don't treat him well at all and you never have. And damn me for not opening my mouth before. That's on me. But no more. I'm not doing it. He's not yours, he's his own man. It's up to him what he does."

Wyatt cheered internally at Lukas's words, thrilled to have him stand up for the two of them. The next moment he was shocked to see Lukas turn and beckon Shy to come out from behind him.

"Shy can make up his own mind. Can't you, Shy?"

Wyatt's blood ran cold. He couldn't ask Shy to make such a choice. Shy was too fragile. He needed time, time away from Grant. Time to heal. And yes, he was afraid that if he was made to pick, Shy might revert to habit and automatically return to what he knew. *Dammit, Lukas, what are you doing?*

Silently, he willed Shy to remain where he was, and for a long moment, he believed that was just what would happen. But slowly, he felt Shy's arms ease away from him, felt the absence of his body as he stepped around Wyatt, toward Grant. Wyatt thought his heart would surely break, lanced with a pain so great it took his breath away, leaving him speechless. But he was powerless to do anything other than watch.

The look of triumph in Grant's eyes was obscene as Shy slowly moved toward him, step by step. As if he was sleepwalking. A look of horror crossed Lukas's face, and he flashed a look toward Wyatt that seemed apologetic. Lot of good that would do now. Wyatt couldn't bear the thought he was losing Shy already, when they'd barely had a chance to explore their new relationship. Right after Shy admitted he loved him. Didn't love trump everything? Didn't love conquer all?

Most of all he couldn't stand the idea that Shy would be hurt again by this man. That was the worst part. He just knew Grant would have the worst possible punishments in mind for what he considered Shy's transgressions. He couldn't bear to know what would be happening just across the street from him. Hot tears threatened to blind him. He reached out for Shy without thinking, a low moan escaping him, but Lukas restrained him.

"He has to choose," he said simply.

Wyatt could do nothing but watch Shy walk away from him, toward Grant. In the back of his mind, he knew Lukas was right, but at the same time his heart said no, and he silently cursed Lukas for doing this.

Suddenly Shy stopped, maybe halfway to Grant. As Wyatt watched in amazement, he straightened himself to his full height, setting his feet apart as if intending to take root there.

"What are you doing? Get over here." Grant was beginning to grow belligerent now. Shy flinched. But he continued to stand his ground.

"Lukas said I need to choose, and that's just what I'm doing," he said, his voice surprisingly calm. "And I choose Wyatt."

Wyatt thought he hadn't heard right. He blinked in amazement, mouth dropping open. Did Shy actually choose him over Grant? Was that possible?

Grant was openly glowering now, his face suffusing a deep red. "What did you just say?" he asked.

"I thought I didn't deserve any better than you," Shy continued, his slender frame beginning to shake slightly. "I thought I must be a really horrible person to receive everything you've ever done to me. What my mother did to me. But then I met Wyatt… and he showed me that I *am* someone who deserves to be treated with respect. To be loved even."

Shy's voice broke, as if choking with sobs, but he held up his hand, as if to stop anyone from interfering. "You have no idea what love even means, Randy. Wyatt does, and now I do too. I love him. I'm going to make a life with him, if he'll have me. I want to make something out of myself, be something other than your doormat. Your servant. Your personal whipping boy."

"You ungrateful little bastard," Grant snarled, all pretense of calm having dropped away. "You *are* mine. I paid for—" He stopped himself suddenly, as if all too aware he was about to admit to something most people would not only find unconscionable but very illegal. And they were far from alone. In fact, Wyatt was surprised to find quite a few people had stopped to listen, drinks in hand. Some looked amused, but most seemed horrified by what they'd been hearing.

"Hey man, leave the kid alone," someone spoke up.

"He made his choice, now live with it" came from someone else. A chorus of murmurs began to grow.

Shy turned and looked back at Wyatt, his eyes speaking volumes. Wyatt held his arms open and Shy ran into them. Wyatt clasped him, stroked his head, murmuring soft words. Grant took two steps in their direction, and he clutched Shy even more tightly. Before Grant could get any closer, Lukas had grabbed his arm.

"Let it go, Randy," he said. "You have a reputation to consider. Think of your company."

The hellish fury on Grant's face was indescribable, almost comic. Under other circumstances, Wyatt would have laughed. But now all he could think of was keeping Shy safe.

"You think you've won some great victory, don't you?" he hissed at Wyatt. "Take him then. I don't care. He means nothing to me. Never did. There are more like him." He turned to glare at Lukas. "Think you're so clever, don't you? Remember that next time we meet."

"Save your threats, I don't see that happening," Lukas said. "I know Bobby's kicked you out of the club. Have a nice life, Randy. Not that you deserve it."

Grant spun about without another word. Those people unlucky enough to be standing behind him parted, allowing him to leave the room as quickly as he could.

The show over, everyone returned to mingling, and appreciating art, and whatever else they'd been doing.

Wyatt regarded Lukas over Shy's bent head. "Thank you," he said. "I wasn't sure you would…."

"Stand up for you?" Lukas shook his head. "After what I said before, I guess I have that coming. I thought you were wrong, I admit it. I figured Shy would only get hurt by being with you. That you weren't thinking clearly. But then, seeing you two together today, and listening to what you both said… I had a lot to think about. And I didn't like myself very much. I knew what he was doing, and I didn't do anything about it. I owe you an apology, Shy. A great big one."

Wyatt kissed the top of Shy's head. Shy turned around, facing Lukas. "It's okay," he said. "I understand. I do. Randy has a way of making people believe he's right even when he's wrong."

"That's why he's so good at what he does," Lukas said. "Wyatt, you can't stay there, of course. Not at Masterson's house. Not now. That's too close to Randy, and there's no telling what he might try if you go back there."

"But I have to," Wyatt protested. "I'm house-sitting, remember? I have an obligation to be there."

"I remember. Don't worry, I'll find someone else. Tell you what, I'm going to take you back so you can grab your stuff. Then I'll find you a hotel, just for tonight. Tomorrow we'll work something out."

"Is that all right with you?" Wyatt asked Shy. He wanted to make sure Shy had a voice in everything that happened to him. He didn't want Shy to ever feel helpless again.

"That sounds good," Shy said.

"All right, let's go then. I'll follow you, so you can leave John's car there, and you can get your stuff, and I'll drive you to a hotel."

Suddenly, the world seemed a much brighter place than it had just a few minutes ago.

CHAPTER SIXTEEN

WYATT AND Shy collected what little stuff they had at Masterson's house—most of that Wyatt's since Shy had brought very little—while Lukas kept an eye out for Grant, in case he decided to make more trouble for them. The house across the street remained dark—no sign of its owner, and the car wasn't in the drive.

Afterward, Lukas drove them to a motel in north St. Louis County, figuring it would be a good idea to put a little distance between them and Grant. They'd stopped along the way and picked up burgers and fries at a fast-food restaurant. Lukas left them with some money, in case they wanted to get something later. A convenience store was just a short walk away, but Lukas cautioned them not to go any farther than that, just to be safe.

"I'll be back tomorrow," Lukas promised as he was leaving. "We'll figure out something more long-term then, but for right now, you should be okay." He gave Wyatt a significant look. It didn't take a rocket scientist to figure out he had something to say… in private.

"Be right back," Wyatt told Shy. "Pick whichever bed you want, doesn't matter to me." He gave Shy a reassuring smile before following Lukas out the door.

"Is something wrong?" Wyatt asked.

"Not wrong, I just want you to remember how fragile Shy is right now. I know you know that"—he held up one hand in a placating manner before Wyatt had a chance to respond—"and I'm not saying you'd hurt him. I'm not blind. I can see how you two feel about each other, and I do remember what it was like to be young and in love. Just… move at his pace, okay?"

"I'd never do anything he didn't want," Wyatt protested. "Trust me."

"I do trust you. If I didn't, you two wouldn't be sharing a motel room, believe me. I'd have separated you and made Shy go with me. I just want you to be prepared to stop if Shy can't handle something, okay? Whether he says anything or not. You'll just have to know when to leave it alone. I can't honestly say I know everything about what happened with Randy and him, but I know enough to think Shy's had a very rough time of it."

Wyatt understood Lukas's concern. In fact, he shared it. He intended to be very gentle with Shy. Sure, he wanted to make love with Shy, but that was far from his only interest in him. Not even his main interest. There was so much more to a relationship than sex—at least he thought there should be. He'd never had one that lasted long enough to test his theory. But he intended to find out with Shy.

"All right then, I'll call you tomorrow." Lukas gave Wyatt a quick hug before pulling back with a self-deprecating chuckle. "You know how us *old* people get. Worry all the time about you young whippersnappers."

Wyatt had to smile at that. "Lukas, you'll never be old. Ornery maybe, but not old."

"Ornery I can live with." Lukas laughed.

Once he'd gone, Wyatt returned inside.

This motel room might not be anywhere near as luxurious as Masterson's place, but Wyatt thought it was perfect, because he was able to be there with Shy. This was a dream come true.

The room contained two double beds. They sat together on one as they ate their dinner and watched a little television. Wyatt couldn't even say what programs they watched. Maybe something with a detective. Or police officers. He was too aware of Shy's proximity to be aware of much else.

Shy had claimed the bed farthest from the door. Wyatt couldn't blame him for that. Probably made him feel a little more secure, no doubt.

"Let me know when you're ready for sleep," Wyatt said. He expected Shy was probably tired, after such a trying day.

"I'm ready for bed now," Shy said, "but I'm not tired."

"Are you hungry? We can walk over to the convenience store and see what they've got."

"I don't want food," Shy replied.

Wyatt shot him a baffled look. "Then what—"

"I want to be with you," Shy said in a low-pitched voice that was already doing things to Wyatt. "I want you to make love to me… please."

"A-are you sure?" Wyatt hadn't expected the question of sex to arise quite so soon, no pun intended, even though they were sharing a motel room. He'd anticipated they'd end up in the same bed, sure, following the pattern they'd established over the last couple of nights, but just to sleep. He discounted Shy's attempted blowjob as nothing more than misdirected gratitude, and an expectation that didn't exist.

But everything had changed, hadn't it? Shy had been set free. He didn't have to answer to Grant any more. Or anyone else. He was his own man now. And he wanted Wyatt to make love to him of his own volition. Wyatt was both ecstatic and apprehensive. He couldn't forget Lukas's parting words. He would *not* hurt Shy, no matter what. He didn't want to take anything between them too quickly. And yet he wanted him… very much.

"I'm quite sure." Shy took Wyatt's hand in his and placed it against his chest. Wyatt could feel the rhythmic thump thump of Shy's heart beneath his palm. "My heart belongs to you already. I've never felt this way before, Wyatt. I'm a little scared, but I know what I want. And what I want is you."

They came together in a gentle kiss. Then another, and another, Wyatt allowing Shy all the freedom he desired. He tasted and nibbled Wyatt's lips in between kisses, and by the time they stopped for breath, Wyatt's lips throbbed, but with pleasure, not pain.

"Can I ask a favor?" Shy asked softly.

"Ask me anything you want."

"Can I touch you?"

Shy's request went straight to Wyatt's heart. He didn't even want to imagine what life with the Keeper must have been like, if Shy had been reduced to asking permission for everything he did. Thank God that was over now, and he'd never have to live under Grant's rule again.

"Would you like to undress me?" Wyatt asked.

"Can I... do you mind... I mean, really?" He seemed embarrassed, the words tumbling awkwardly from his lips. "It's just that I couldn't... he never...." He broke off, casting his gaze to the floor.

Wyatt tried not to show his anger, although inwardly he writhed at the continuing evidence of the mind-trip Grant had laid on Shy. Grant had probably never touched Shy in any way that was not sexual, or meant to cause pain, much less allowed Shy to touch him except at his direction, for his pleasure. No tenderness, no mutual exploration. Certainly no love.

For a moment Wyatt flared with anger at the thought of the man he'd dubbed the Keeper. Then he pushed that away. No sense in thinking about what was. He needed to concentrate on the here and now, and showing Shy that what happened between two consulting adults who cared about one another was a beautiful thing.

Wyatt tilted Shy's face up toward him once more. "I would love to have you undress me." He was rewarded with a tremulous smile. "And just for the record, you can touch me however you want. As much or as little. I give you my permission."

Shy's face clouded slightly, and Wyatt could have kicked himself. Should he have used a different word? Did that one remind him of Randy in some way? Damn, he had to tread so carefully, but this was all so new to him. Shy's face cleared quickly, and his smile was a little more confident.

"Good to know," he said. "You have my permission too."

Wyatt was sure that Shy'd never had the opportunity to make such an offer before, that Grant had simply taken what he wanted and Shy had to follow his orders without question. This was a major step for him. Wyatt's heart swelled with pride.

"What would you like me to do?" Wyatt asked.

"Raise your arms?" Shy said, and Wyatt obeyed.

Very carefully, Shy pulled Wyatt's shirt up his chest, and then over his arms and off. He shook the garment out, folded it carefully and set it on the extra bed. He turned back toward Wyatt, his eyes seeming to drink him in. As though mesmerized by the sight, Shy reached out hesitantly, trailing his fingertips over first one nipple, then the other. They pebbled at Shy's touch, becoming hard dusky nubs.

"That feels good," Wyatt encouraged him.

Shy nodded, as if satisfied with the result, looking Wyatt over. "Shoes should come next," he decided, "before the pants. Maybe you should sit on the bed? I think that would be easier."

"Your wish is my command." Wyatt took a seat near the end of the bed, but made no move to do anything else, placing himself completely under Shy's control. Shy knelt at Wyatt's feet. He lifted one leg so that Wyatt's foot rested on Shy's thigh. He unlaced, then removed the tennis shoe, followed by the sock, then repeated the process with the other leg.

Wyatt was surprised when Shy didn't immediately set his foot back on the floor. He stroked it instead, almost a massage, kneading the top of Wyatt's foot with a skillful touch. Wyatt closed his eyes and gave in to the luxurious sensation. No one had ever touched him like that before. Turned out Shy was full of surprises.

Shy continued to caress Wyatt's foot before placing it carefully onto the floor. Using Wyatt's thighs for leverage, he rose from his knees, and after a moment of hesitation, reached for Wyatt's belt. He unbuckled it and drew it slowly through the loops. Wyatt loved Shy's expression, the look of concentration as he focused on removing Wyatt's clothes. Wyatt was already so hard he felt as though he might burst. As Shy pulled his zipper down, his swollen cock sprang out, grateful to be freed. Shy wrapped his fingers around it, and Wyatt couldn't help but moan.

"You feel so good," Shy said. He gently brushed his thumb across the head, from which precum already drizzled. Wyatt was disappointed when he released him and turned his attention to pulling his jeans down instead. Once he pulled the pants down Wyatt's legs and off, he folded them and set them with the rest.

"Should I go ahead and… I mean, do you want me to strip?" Shy asked.

While Wyatt would certainly have appreciated such a sight, he suspected that was something Grant would have him do, make Shy disrobe as part of his entertainment. Maybe some other time. Tonight he wanted to minister to Shy, show him how enjoyable shared pleasure was.

"I'd like to do that myself, if you don't mind."

Wyatt savored the removal of every piece of clothing, kissing and caressing every inch of flesh as it was revealed. Once Shy was naked also, they fell onto the bed of mutual accord and kissed, rubbing their bodies together, as if they couldn't get close enough. This felt so good, felt so right.… Wyatt was afraid if he didn't pace himself, he'd release too soon, and that would be a shame.

When Shy pulled back, Wyatt was afraid he'd done something wrong, although he didn't have an idea what that might be. But Shy's question put his mind at ease.

"Do we have lube?"

Wyatt mentally kicked himself for not thinking of that. Good thing Shy remembered. But did he have anything? Or would they have to put their plans on hold? That would be frustrating but not the end of the world. He remembered tossing a bunch of stuff from the bathroom into his bag in his rush to get out of the house. Maybe there was something there they could use.

"I think there might be. Let me take a look." He gave Shy a quick kiss before he rolled off the bed, hunting for his suitcase. There it was, right where he'd left it on their arrival. He tossed it onto the extra bed and quickly unzipped it, checking the compartments for something they could use for lubrication.

Voila! Apparently he'd had lube left over from the last time he'd needed it. He raised it aloft in triumph for Shy to see. Good thing he'd found it, or their plans would have been cut short. No way was he willing to take Shy dry. That would have been painful, and that was so not happening.

He climbed back onto the bed. Uncapping the bottle, he squirted some of the contents onto the fingers of one hand and rubbed them together, letting the heat of his body warm the liquid a little. "Are you sure you're ready?" He wanted to give Shy a chance to change his mind. Although he hoped he wouldn't, he could live with it, if that was Shy's decision. He refused to pressure him in any way. He wasn't Randy Grant.

"I'm not a virgin, Wyatt," Shy reminded him with a small smile.

"I know," Wyatt said. "I just want you to know you have a choice, that's all."

"I appreciate that," Shy said. "I do. And I choose you." He crooked his finger and beckoned to Wyatt, at the same time spreading his legs provocatively. Wyatt found he could do no less than obey.

Shy pulled Wyatt down until their lips met, crashing their mouths together in a searing kiss as he rubbed against Wyatt needily. Wyatt didn't try to guide or direct, allowing Shy the freedom to move at his own pace, to express himself as he wished.

At last Wyatt drew back, reluctantly breaking the kiss. Shy's lips were sweet, but he had other, more pressing needs right now. Wyatt took his lube-coated hand and teased Shy's pucker, circling it before sliding one finger inside, followed by a second one.

Shy gasped. "More!" he begged, and Wyatt carefully added a third finger, scissoring them inside of Shy as he worked at stretching him.

"Need you," Shy moaned, and the look in his big blue eyes left no doubt how much he wanted Wyatt.

Wyatt reached inside Shy for that particular bundle of nerves that he knew from experience gave such pleasure, prodding them. Shy yelped when he touched him, and for a moment, Wyatt was afraid he'd hurt him. Shy's reaction quickly told him otherwise.

"Omigod, how'd you do that?" Shy arched his back, digging his heels into the bed. "However you did, can you please do it again?"

Why was Wyatt not surprised that Shy had never had his prostate touched? Further proof, not that he needed any, that Grant was an utter pig and completely selfish.

"That's part of you, love," Wyatt said, touching him again. He was gratified at the look of sheer ecstasy that passed over Shy's face. "Something all men have. It's called the prostate. Kind of like a woman's G spot."

"That… that's amazing," Shy said. Precum dripped in earnest from his hard cock. "*You're* amazing."

To Wyatt's surprise, Shy reached between them and grasped Wyatt's slick cock.

"I'm ready for you *now*," Shy said, removing his hand in preparation.

Wyatt didn't need to be told twice. He entered Shy smoothly and completely, sheathing himself inside all that liquid heat. Shy wrapped his legs around Wyatt's middle, crossing his ankles and resting his feet against the small of Wyatt's back.

Wyatt intended to be gentle their first time, but Shy was making that resolution difficult to keep. He snapped his hips in a steady rhythm, and Wyatt could do no less than follow his lead. Wet flesh slapped against wet flesh, Wyatt burying himself as deep inside Shy as he could get.

They fused their mouths again, breathing their hunger jointly, as if they could not get enough of each other. Shy fisted his hands into Wyatt's curls, clutching tightly. The pain only served to heighten their experience. Wyatt felt as though something electric was passing from him to Shy and back again, as though a circuit had been completed between them. Reaching for Shy's hard cock, he pumped it in time to his own thrusts inside him. He didn't know how long he would last at this rate, but he was determined to make sure Shy found his release first.

Shy's slender cock pulsed in Wyatt's hand, his mewls of pleasure barely audible. Eyes closed and lips invitingly parted, he managed to look both debauched and innocent. As Shy's moans increased and his body vibrated, Wyatt suspected he was close to his climax, and squeezed even harder.

"Oh God, Wyatt," Shy began, but barely had the words crossed his lips when he came, pumping streams of fluid that covered Wyatt's hand, and spattered both their chests in stickiness. Shy's muscles contracted tightly around Wyatt's thrusting cock, eliciting moans of his own.

"Come inside me," Shy begged. "Make me yours."

Shy's sultry voice as he urged Wyatt to his orgasm, combined with the way his walls gripped Wyatt, squeezing him, was all he needed to fall over the precipice, crying out Shy's name as he came. He came hard and fast, harder than he thought he'd ever come before, inside of Shy.

Shy pulled Wyatt down so their mouths met once more, deepening the kiss, holding on for dear life, until Wyatt felt he didn't know where one left off and the other began. Wyatt couldn't come forever. With a last shudder, he rolled over slightly, so he wouldn't be too heavy on Shy, who burrowed into his arms, his face buried against Wyatt's chest.

Wyatt stroked the damp blond hair gently, letting his breathing even out. Words couldn't even begin to describe how he felt. He was happy, elated, exhausted, exuberant, triumphant… and most of all, he was in love. Head over heels, happily in love. In a short time, Shy had become everything to him. He wanted to build a life with him. Make a new beginning for both of them.

"I love you, Shy," he whispered softly, receiving a murmured response in return. Shy turned his face up toward Wyatt and repeated what he'd said.

"I love you too, Wyatt." He stared directly into Wyatt's eyes, and Wyatt could tell something was running around in his mind. Something troubling?

"Can I ask you something?" Shy said at last.

"Of course. Ask me anything. What do you want to know?"

"Why did you come over?"

"What do you mean?" Wyatt gave Shy a puzzled look.

"That first day. When you came across the street and asked was something wrong. What made you do that?"

That was a fair question. Why had he stuck his nose where it didn't belong, when he'd made no effort to meet any of the neighbors before? He'd be lying if he said it was a neighborly gesture on his part. But simple curiosity didn't exactly explain it either.

The only explanation he had was tenuous at best, but it's what he had.

"Something drew me," he said. "I dunno. I saw you there, saw you washing that car, over and over. And something inside of me said *go over there*. I didn't know what I was going to say or do. I half expected to be told to mind my own business. But I had to try."

Shy released a long-held sigh, his fingers playing with the curly hairs on Wyatt's chest. "You want to know something?"

"What's that?" Wyatt asked.

"I'm really glad you did." They kissed again and again and again, got up long enough to take a shower together, then headed back to bed to make love again, all night long.

JULIE LYNN HAYES was reading at the age of two and writing by the age of nine and always wanted to be a writer when she grew up. Two marriages, five children, and more than forty years later, that is still her dream. She blames her younger daughters for introducing her to yaoi and the world of M/M love, a world which has captured her imagination and her heart and fueled her writing in ways she'd never dreamed of before. She especially loves stories of two men finding true love and happiness in one another's arms and is a great believer in happily ever after.

She lives in St. Louis with her daughter Sarah and her cat Ramesses, loves books and movies, and hopes to be a world traveler someday. She enjoys crafts, such as crocheting and cross-stitch, knitting and needlepoint, and loves to cook. While working a temporary day job, she continues to write her books and stories and reviews, which she posts in various places on the internet. Her family thinks she is a bit off, but she doesn't mind. Marching to the beat of one's own drummer is a good thing, after all.

Blog: julielynnhayes.blogspot.com
Email: tothemax.wolf@gmail.com

BE MY ALIEN

MOONLIT SKIES

M.A. CHURCH
JULIE LYNN HAYES

Moonlit Skies: Book One

A man too busy for love…

Reed owns an upscale men's boutique with a naughty back room. While making a late delivery to a client, he runs into Taz.

A man on a disastrous date…

When Taz agreed to come to Earth on a date, he didn't expect to be dumped and left with no way home. Then he falls into Reed's arms—literally.

A coffee date soon becomes a trip back to Reed's apartment. But when Taz's stripes begin to show, Reed discovers Taz comes from a planet far, far away.

Reed never believed aliens existed, but he's facing one now. What in the world is he going to do?

www.dreamspinnerpress.com

BE MY HUMAN

MOONLIT SKIES: BOOK TWO

JULIE LYNN HAYES
M.A. CHURCH

Sequel to *Be My Alien*
Moonlit Skies: Book Two

Reed and Taz are still adjusting to their new lives together when a medical emergency sends them flying down to Florida on short notice. Not quite the way Reed pictured introducing Taz to his family. Reed's sister, Rene, welcomes the outgoing Taz with open arms, and the kittenish alien charms Reed's parents.

But someone isn't quite so enamored of Reed's boyfriend—his homophobic older brother Jacob seems determined to be as unpleasant as possible, and he's making their visit very uncomfortable. The sudden appearance of Reed's controlling ex releases a flood of insecurity and bad memories.

Reed begins to doubt himself, and his ability to love and be loved in return. When strange items begin appearing out of nowhere, he wonders if he's being stalked, or is he just paranoid? What can Taz do to prove to Reed that he's more than enough man for this alien?

www.dreamspinnerpress.com

Rose and Thorne: Book One

Vinnie Delarosa and Ethan Thorne are partners—on and off the clock. Federal undercover detectives, they're part of a covert task force designed to promote goodwill between the feds and local authorities. They lend an unobtrusive helping hand wherever it's needed. No credit required.

Vinnie and Ethan work primarily in the Southeast region of the United States and live together in Richmond, Virginia. A mugger problem brings them to Roanoke, where Vinnie is thrown out as bait to catch the man who's been snatching purses in a city park, but they end up with more than they bargained for. Why is Vinnie always the one who has to wear the dress? Ethan says it's because Vinnie looks much prettier in a skirt. How can he argue with that?

Expecting to return to Richmond afterward, Vinnie and Ethan find themselves assigned a new case instead. They are to go undercover at The Stroll, one of the biggest gay nightclubs in Roanoke. Someone is terrorizing both the customers and the performers. Could they be dealing with a hate crime? Someone has to protect the drag queens of Roanoke, so it's Vinnie and Ethan to the rescue!

www.dreamspinnerpress.com

Civil War
and
Broken Hearts

Julie
Lynn
Hayes

Rose and Thorne: Book Two

Hollywood comes to Roanoke when a major film studio announces they're shooting part of their Civil War film at a local plantation. Vinnie is dismayed to discover the lead actress is none other than the beautiful Caroline St. Clair. Ethan and Vinnie met her in LA the previous Halloween, and Vinnie still hates her for hitting on his man. Ethan reassures his partner that Roanoke is big enough for all of them to coexist without running into one another.

But Fate has it in for Vinnie and Ethan, and they're assigned to a new case involving the actress. Vinnie has no choice—he has to play nice. It's small consolation that his new undercover identity involves Hollywood heartthrob Troy McGarrett, who is very handsome and openly gay. Troy also isn't shy about letting Vinnie know he finds him attractive.

Jealousy abounds, and time is not on Vinnie and Ethan's side. If they don't solve the case before the film shoot is done, there's a good chance they'll be separated for the first time since they were partnered. Assuming Vinnie doesn't kill Caroline St. Clair himself.

www.dreamspinnerpress.com

Family Ties
and
Family Lies

Julie
Lynn
Hayes

Rose and Thorne: Book Three

Secrets is a dirty word when it comes to relationships. What you don't say can not only hurt you, it can bite you in the butt.

After almost five years together, Vinnie and Ethan have a policy of don't ask, don't tell. But unspoken questions between them are a ticking time bomb, waiting to explode. An innocent remark by a friend starts an insecure Vinnie wondering about things he never considered before… such as why he hasn't met Ethan's family. Is he the love of Ethan's life or just his dirty little secret? And what hasn't he told Ethan about his own past?

An emergency phone call from Ethan's twin sister sends them rushing to Georgia. In order to be with Ethan, Vinnie conforms to what Ethan's family expects by being something he is not. Not everything is what it seems as Vinnie and Ethan work to redefine what family means to each of them.

Sometimes the ties that bind are the ones that might just break you.

www.dreamspinnerpress.com

FOR

MORE

OF THE

BEST

GAY

ROMANCE

dreamspinnerpress.com

www.ingramcontent.com/pod-product-compliance
Lightning Source LLC
Chambersburg PA
CBHW060100260626
47160CB00005B/1738